Angus Adams and the Missing Pro Surfer

The Free-Range Kid Mysteries Book 2

Lee. M. Winter

ISBN: 1530303923
ISBN-13: 978-1530303922

DEDICATION

To Clancy and Leo

CONTENTS

ACKNOWLEDGMENTS

Thank you to Mariela Reiss (www.asapediting.com)

1 THE JERK

Angus glanced over his shoulder. A big swell was coming. He paddled like mad and felt the wave lift his board. An awesome right-hander. Okay, wait for it…now! Leaping up, he gripped the waxy board with his feet. If he could just stay upright for four seconds he'd have a new personal best.

What the…? From nowhere, another rider appeared on the lip of the wave. Right on top of him. Angus tried to pull back but couldn't. With a sickening crunch they collided in a jumble of arms, legs, and boards, one of which smacked hard against his head. Then the ocean took over to show who was boss. Dragged down and pounded against the bottom (*was this sand or concrete?*) Angus lost track of which way was up, rolled over and over like a sock in a washing machine and gave himself up for dead. Twenty desperate seconds later he surfaced in the shallows, spluttering and gasping for breath.

"You stupid little idiot!" The other surfer stood over him. "What do you think you were doing? Stay out of the way of the *real* surfers, mate, or go back to kindergarten."

"S…sorry," Angus spluttered. It was hard to talk given that he'd just almost drowned.

"You will be if you do it again, grommet. I'll snap your board in half." With that, the guy turned and headed back out.

Angus rubbed his head. He was relieved to see the board still strapped to his ankle. His friends, Hamish and Bodhi, rushed into the water.

"Crikey. You alright?" said Hamish (as usual, doing his best Steve Irwin, Crocodile Hunter, impersonation). "We didn't think you were going to come up."

"Yeah, I'm okay. I think."

"We saw that guy yelling at you. What a jerk," said Bodhi. "*He* totally dropped in on *you*."

"Yeah, well. I guess I should have stayed out of the way," said Angus. "Here's your board back, thanks. I think I'll just sit on the sand for a while."

Bodhi took her board and paddled away. Angus and Hamish turned for the beach.

"The Helicopter has drinks and snacks," said Hamish. They made their way to a lady sitting under a bright yellow beach umbrella. Hamish's mother was very careful about keeping her pale Scottish skin out of the sun. Hamish called her the 'Helicopter' as she tended to be a bit overprotective, hovering over him constantly. Strongly in her favour, however, was her considerable skill in baking delicious treats. And she was always very generous with them. Especially to Angus, believing he could use some 'fattening up'.

"Eat the wee cupcakes, boys," she said reaching for a huge Tupperware container, "the icing's no' holding up in the heat. Hamish don't be shy with the sunscreen, you know how easily you burn. And where's your hat, lad?"

"Thanks, Mrs McLeod," Angus said, taking a cake. He dropped down onto his towel and surveyed the beach. It was packed.

And why wouldn't it be? They were at Snapper Rocks at Rainbow Bay on the Gold Coast; home of the Quick Silver Pro Surfing event due to start in only five days.

Every man and his dog was here staking out the best bits of beach and the best apartments and holiday houses to catch the world-class surfers doing their thing. The star-spotting was awesome. Just this morning they'd seen Kelly Slater in the water, and yesterday Mick Fanning in the surf club carpark (it was his home turf, after all).

Hamish had sworn Mick had winked at him.

"You're kidding yourself. He just had sand in his eye," Angus had said.

But Hamish was adamant. "I'm telling you, he winked at me."

"Look, he's still rubbing his eye," said Angus, but Mick was already lost in the throng on the beach.

"He winked, swear on my mother's life."

"Don't sacrifice your mother for nothing. There was no wink. No one winks anymore. Winking's totally 1990s."

"What?"

"I'm serious. When was the last time someone

winked at you, before this one, which wasn't one anyway?"

Hamish paused.

"See, you've got nothing. The only winkers are weird old uncles who tell not-very-funny jokes and then wink at you so you know when to pretend to laugh."

"You're insane," said Hamish. "I totally stand by my assertion that I received a wink from Mick Fanning."

Then Hamish had a thong blow-out and stubbed his toe, so the wink debate was suspended without a clear winner.

The apartment high-rises had cast long-fingered shadows over the sand by the time Bodhi came dripping from the surf. They packed up and trudged to the pebbled walkway, loaded with boards, bags and the umbrella. Mrs McLeod left them at the outdoor shower to rinse off while she took a load to her car.

Bodhi's father, Mr Taylor, had invited both boys to stay at his beach house for a week of the school holidays. He'd been left with a spare bedroom when Taj, Bodhi's older brother, couldn't come due to starting a new job. But only Angus's parents had agreed. Hamish had begged and pleaded; *it's only one week, it'll be like I'm at school camp, Angus's parents are fine with it,* all to no avail. In the end it wasn't a big deal as the McLeods decided to stay in a nearby apartment.

Angus tried to play it down to Hamish but staying at Bodhi's beach house *was* totally epic. Not only was it a stone's throw from the surf but this week it was also home to two of the pro surfers actually competing in the big event. Leo and Nate were family friends of the Taylors.

Hanging out. With pro surfers. In a beach house. For seven days.

Epic.

They had to wait their turn to use the shower. The pathway was busy with fitness freaks, late afternoon strollers and families still coming to and from the beach.

Finally the shower was free and Hamish went to move in. A little kid on a scooter lost control and veered off the path right at him. Hamish jumped away, lost his balance and fell into a surfboard leaning against the fence. The board crashed to the ground. Hamish immediately went to pick it up.

"Touch that board and I'll break your arm!" It was the surfer jerk again. Yanking his board away from Hamish, he said, "You moron. If you've damaged this board…yeah, look, right there…there's a ding!"

The jerk yelled and ranted. Hamish shrank back and tried to apologise but that only seemed to enrage the jerk further. People were starting to stop and stare.

"DO YOU KNOW WHAT THIS BOARD'S WORTH? DO YOU KNOW WHO I AM?"

"It was an accident," said Angus, stepping forward in Hamish's defence. This guy was way out of line.

"What? *You* again? This *is* a kindergarten outing for idiot grommets."

"Hey, Dylan, chill dude, they're just kids." It was Leo, and he had Nate with him, boards under their arms, heading for the surf. Obviously, they knew this Dylan guy.

"The board's fine, dude," said Nate to the furious Dylan. "And it's not even your best one."

At that moment Mrs McLeod pulled up at the curb and Hamish scrambled for a quick getaway. Angus couldn't blame him. Hamish puffed on his inhaler as the car pulled away.

The jerk, Dylan, took a step towards Angus and pointed a finger at him. "I'm warning you, kid. Stay out of my way."

2 GONE

Angus and Bodhi cut through the surf club carpark. Angus, starving despite the cupcakes, was thinking about pizza when Bodhi grabbed his arm and said,

"Look over there."

It was the surfer jerk, Dylan, with an older guy. The older man was right up in his face, stabbing a finger at him, very unhappy about something. Dylan just stood there looking at his feet.

The older guy raised his voice, "Do you want to win

this thing or not? Answer me!"

Dylan muttered something they couldn't catch.

"Then smarten up your attitude, son. I've spent *a lot* of money getting you here. Don't blow it now. Do you hear me!"

No answer from Dylan.

"I said, DO YOU HEAR ME!"

Dylan's head snapped up. "Yeah! Yes, okay, Dad, whatever."

"Don't you 'whatever' me, son!"

Angus nudged Bodhi and they kept moving through the carpark.

"Being a jerk must run in the family," said Bodhi.

***

Mr Taylor had written a beach house cooking roster but tonight was 'take-away night' or 'take-out night' as Nate, an American, said. So Angus got his pizza. Everyone ate on the deck. The evening was mild and they were close enough to hear the ocean roll in as the sun slowly sank behind the mountains in the west.

Angus was on his third slice of meat-lovers as Bodhi told her Dad about the surf-rage incident. The first one, in the water.

"It happened so fast, he didn't even have time to fall

off," she said. Angus would have said 'ha, ha' had his mouth not been so full.

"Dylan can be a jerk sometimes," said Leo, taking a slice of pepperoni.

"We noticed," said Angus, after finally swallowing.

Leo explained that Dylan was a pro surfer, a rookie like they were, in town for the competition. As grommets, Leo and Bodhi's brother had surfed with Dylan at the same Sydney beaches.

"His Dad's a hard case," said Nate. "Puts pressure on him to win, you know?" Nate's Californian accent made everything he said even cooler than it already was.

Mr Taylor filled water cups from a jug. To Angus, he said, "How's the head now, mate?"

Angus felt his skull. "Okay, but I've got a lump the size of a small golf ball."

"There's no such thing as a small golf ball," said Bodhi, wiping her mouth with a napkin. "Golf balls are all the same size. There aren't big ones and small ones."

"Okay, then it's the size of a macadamia nut. Is that acceptable?" said Angus.

"A *what* nut?" said Nate.

"Macadamia," said Leo. He put on a TV presenter's voice. "Native to Australia, one generally finds thriving macadamia crops in South Eastern Queensland and Northern New South Wales. Jeez, get an education, why don't ya?"

"I'm pretty sure they're grown in California, too, Nate," said Mr Taylor.

"No way," said Nate. "Or *I'm* pretty sure I would have heard of an academia nut before now."

"*Macadamia!*" said the others all together.

"Google it, dude," said Leo.

***

Angus stuck his head in the door of Leo's downstairs sleep-out to say goodnight. The surfer was on his knees, bent over his board applying wax in long, smooth strokes. On the bed was an open display-folder. The top page showed a close up shot of Leo doing an aerial.

"Have a look if you like," he said. Angus sat on the bed and flicked through the incredible photos.

"When did you know you were good enough to go pro?"

Leo laughed. "I still don't. But I guess we're about to find out."

Angus turned the pages. "They reckon you're the favourite. To win the rookie section, at least." This year there was a new section of the competition open only to those on their first year of the pro circuit.

"Yeah. Well. We'll see. Competition's stiff." Leo kept working over the board.

He was being modest. There'd been a big write-up in the local paper all about Leo; how he'd won his last six amateur comps, how talented he was, how everyone was tipping him to win on Saturday.

Angus looked at a photograph of Leo coming out of a barrel. "What does it take to get so good?" he asked. On the beach, he often sat and watched the pro surfers carve up the waves and perform re-entries and aerials, making it look effortless.

"A lot of hard work," said Leo.

"Where would someone start if, you know, they wanted to end up a pro?"

"You mean you?" Leo stopped waxing and looked up.

"Well, no, I mean, yeah, sure it'd be awesome but I doubt I'll ever be good enough."

Leo shrugged. "I don't see why not. If you're prepared to work hard. But learning to surf is only one part of it. First, you have to understand tides, rips, waves, and water safety." He went back to waxing as he spoke. "Then you need to learn about surf etiquette.

Who has right of way on a wave, that kind of thing."

"I think I had a lesson in that, today," said Angus, feeling the lump on his head.

"From what I heard, it was Dylan who was in the wrong. Forget him. He can be a big-headed twit."

"So what do you use this folder for?" asked Angus.

"That's my portfolio. Wherever *I* go, *it* goes. Any surfer looking to go pro needs one. Surfing the comps is really expensive. Nate's lucky. His dad is loaded. Super rich, in fact, so he doesn't ever have to worry about costs." Nate's dad, some kind of bigwig business man, was flying in from the US tomorrow.

Leo continued, "But the rest of us need to find sponsors, and to do that you have to market yourself. That portfolio has all the professional photos of me surfing. There's a DVD in there, too. You never know when you'll want to pull it out and show a potential sponsor. Like I said, I never go anywhere without it."

"A sponsorship deal's part of the prize this weekend, isn't it?" asked Angus, closing the folder.

"Yep, sure is," said Leo.

"Well, good luck," said Angus, getting up off the bed. "Awesome board, by the way."

"Yeah, my Forget Me Not. She's a beauty, isn't she?

Something else I never go anywhere without. Although I do have another one at the folk's cabin up the mountain. That one's dinged up a bit, though."

"Okay. Well, I guess I better go to bed." Angus walked to the door. Leo looked up.

"I'm hitting the waves at six, mate, if you wanna come? Happy to give you a few pointers."

A surfing lesson from a pro. *Beyond* e*pic!*

"Sure! Cool!"

But when morning came it was clear there would be no lesson.

Because there was no Leo.

3 FOUR DAYS TO GO

Angus and Bodhi rapped on Leo's door at exactly 6 a.m. Bodhi wasn't going to miss out on this lesson from a pro. No answer, but the door swung open under Angus's knuckles. Leo wasn't there. The bed looked unslept in. The portfolio was on the bedside table and his surfboard, his treasured Forget Me Not, leaned against the wall.

A piece of paper lay on the floor by the door. Bodhi picked it up. Something was printed on it. She scanned it with widening eyes.

"Listen to this," she said and read aloud, "After a lot of thought, I've decided not to compete in the competition this weekend. The pressure and stress have been too much for me. I'm going away to be on my own for a while. Don't worry about me. Leo."

They looked at each other.

"What? That doesn't make any sense," said Angus. Leo had been fine last night. He wouldn't just up and leave, would he?

"I better show Dad," said Bodhi.

***

Everyone gathered in the kitchen. Word had spread through the house that Leo was gone. Mr Taylor read the note aloud.

When he finished, he said, "Well, that's a real shame. Didn't see it coming, myself. Nate, did you know he was stressed?"

"No," said Nate, shaking his head. "This is totally weird. He *wasn't* stressed. He was looking forward to competing. He knew he had it in the bag." Everyone stood, looking at each other.

"Well," said Mr Taylor, putting the note on the counter. "Obviously, he was hiding it well. I guess we have to respect his decision. Can't do much else."

"Shouldn't we look for him, at least?" said Angus. He didn't want to be disrespectful to Mr Taylor but the whole thing just seemed too strange to just do *nothing*.

"He's eighteen, Angus. Legally an adult," said Mr Taylor. "If he wants to take off then that's his business."

"Well, we should tell his parents, shouldn't we?" Angus said.

"Can't," said Nate. "Leo told me they're trekking through Nepal for the next two weeks. No phone signal, no email, no communicado. Zip."

"Where could he have gone?" said Bodhi to no one in particular. "It looked like all his things were still in his room."

"Hard to say," said Nate, shrugging. "Back to Sydney, I guess. Or maybe to his parents' cabin on Mount Tamborine."

"He mentioned a cabin last night," said Angus, remembering Leo had said he had another board stored there.

"A bunch of us stayed there for a weekend a while back," Nate added. "He might have gone up there, to chill for a bit, I guess." Tamborine was one of the mountains in the Gold Coast Hinterland.

"There you go then," said Mr Taylor, putting the note

on the counter. "If that's where he is, then I'd be surprised if he's not back before the competition starts. Let's leave him alone for a couple of days and let him get his head together. Now, who's hungry? How about bacon, eggs, and orange juice?" Mr Taylor opened the fridge and busied himself in it.

No one said much over breakfast. Angus did his best to eat but found he didn't have much of an appetite. The whole thing with Leo was really weird. Would he seriously have been waxing his board and suggesting lessons for the morning if he was planning to leave that very night?

After breakfast he pulled Bodhi aside. "What do you think?" he asked her. "About Leo?"

"I'm not sure. I guess it's possible he might have been feeling the pressure and none of us picked up on it."

"But?" said Angus

"But, I just can't see it. If anything, he was more relaxed and happy than any of the others."

"That's what I think, too. And then there's the note. Do you think there's anything strange about the note?"

Bodhi thought for a moment. "He didn't sign it," she said. "I mean with a pen or anything. And it kind of seems a bit formal, to me. Printing it out like that. Why didn't he just write it on a piece of paper?"

"And there's no printer in this house," said Angus. "Not even a computer. It's a holiday house." Bodhi's eyes widened.

"That's right! I didn't even think of that. Of course, there's no printer here."

"So we're supposed to believe he went to all the trouble of going somewhere and printing out a note rather than just write it on a piece of paper. I doubt it."

"What do you think happened then?" said Bodhi.

"I don't know," Angus said. "But last night he showed me his portfolio and told me how important it is to him and how he *never* goes anywhere without it, and —"

"And it's still here in his room!" finished Bodhi, "I saw it myself."

"Exactly," said Angus.

"You know, there's big prize money this weekend for the winning rookie pro. Like, a hundred and fifty thousand dollars," Bodhi said.

Angus raised his eyebrows. "They don't make that much, do they?"

"Not usually, but this year some rich old ex-surfer

has put up extra prize money to help the newbies get a leg up. And there's the sponsorship deal, too. That's worth even bigger dollars."

Angus thought about this. "Everyone's expecting Leo to win," he said.

"But he can't win if he doesn't compete."

"So maybe *someone* doesn't want him to compete," Angus said.

"Are you saying you think he's been kidnapped? To get him out of the way for someone else to win?"

Angus sighed. "I don't know. But what if that *is* what's happened? Leo's out there somewhere, desperately needing help and we don't bother to do anything?"

They went back to Bodhi's dad and tried to convince him that things just didn't add up.

When they'd finished pleading their case, he said,"Guys, I agree it's strange. And we're all a bit shocked, and maybe feeling a little bad that none of us realised how Leo was feeling, but strange things happen all the time. That doesn't mean there's anything sinister going on. I've tried calling his phone. He's not answering but I left a message. I'm sure he'll get in touch when he's ready."

Angus and Bodhi started to talk at the same time. Mr Taylor held up his hand and sighed.

"Okay, look, I have a mate in the police force at Coolangatta. I suppose I could phone him and see what he thinks, if it will make you feel better."

They watched him make the call. He told his policeman friend what they knew about Leo's disappearance and read him the note. Then he walked with the phone outside and down the steps to Leo's sleep-out, still talking to the policeman. Angus and Bodhi followed along behind like puppies, trying not to miss a word.

Inside Leo's room, Mr Taylor said into the phone, "No, I'm in there now and it's neat and tidy...righto then. Okay, thanks for that, Rob. Have to catch up soon, how's the wife?...Good, good. Okay, cheers, mate." He hung up and turned to them.

"Like I thought, he says Leo's eighteen, he's left a note, and, importantly, there's no sign of a disturbance here in his room and none of us heard anything last night."

"But —"Angus started. Mr Taylor held up his hand again.

"Rob, my detective friend, said that it's too early yet

21

to do anything. If he hasn't turned up, say, by the end of next week, and no one's heard from him, then they might look into it."

"But he'll have missed the competition by then," said Bodhi, "There're only four days to go."

"That's just how it is, love," said Mr Taylor.

He went back upstairs, leaving Angus and Bodhi to consider things.

"I still don't like it," said Angus. "Just because his room's neat doesn't mean someone didn't force him out, or trick him or something." Being a converted sleep-out, Leo's room had its own entrance from the yard. They both agreed it would be possible for someone to come and go without anyone upstairs hearing.

Angus took one last look at the room. There was something different from last night. Leo's portfolio was on the bedside table rather than the bed where Angus had left it. And something else was different. Angus went over to the table. Something had been drawn on the portfolio's cover. A circle. And inside it was something that looked like a leaf. It had been drawn in red pen.

"This wasn't on here last night," he said.

Bodhi shrugged. "So Leo drew it last night before leaving?"

"No chance. He went on about how important this folder is. No way would he have doodled over it."

"Looks a bit Hawaiian, don't you think?" said Bodhi, studying the doodle.

"Yeah, maybe," agreed Angus. "I wonder if it means anything."

Bodhi shrugged.

Not knowing what else to do, they left the room. Outside, something on the ground beneath a bush caught Angus's eye. He reached for it.

"Look at this," he said.

4 A JOB

It was a paper napkin. From a restaurant. Folded, as though it had been in someone's pocket. Angus opened it out.

"The Sea Shanty," he read. He and Bodhi peered at it. 'The Sea Shanty' was printed at the top. Under the logo someone had written "Quick Silver Pro $150k" and underlined it. In red pen.

Angus looked at Bodhi. "I think someone *did* come here last night. And whoever it was drew that picture on Leo's portfolio *and* dropped this napkin out here."

"Angus, Leo could have done both those things himself." Bodhi was always so practical. "And the napkin could've blown in from the street," she added. "That's what Dad will say, anyhow."

"But it's in red pen just like the drawing on the folder. That would be big coincidence if it just blew in off the street."

"Red pen isn't that rare, Angus."

"True. But still. Have you heard of The Sea Shanty?"

Bodhi hadn't. They showed the napkin to Mr Taylor and Nate to rule out that it had been dropped by anyone in the house. Neither knew anything about it.

"Probably blew in from the street," said Mr Taylor.

***

Angus's was frustrated that he didn't have his iPad to Google The Sea Shanty. It had been a challenge from Mr Taylor that the kids spend the week device-free. Angus hadn't minded since he intended to pretty much just hang at the beach most days, but now it was a nuisance.

"I'm going over to Hamish's apartment," he told Bodhi. "He can look it up on his laptop." Not staying at Bodhi's, Hamish wasn't bound by the 'no device' challenge. "Want to come?"

But Bodhi decided to hang around the house, just in case they heard from Leo.

Angus put on his cross-trainers. Might as well run the four blocks. It was a sunny morning but the wind was up already. Good thing it was at his back. He crossed the street and jogged past the little Italian café that sat across the street from the beach house. A grey-haired man was busy setting up outdoor tables and umbrellas, whistling as he worked. He sung out a cheery "Good-a-morning!" as Angus passed.

Hamish was eating cereal in front of the television when Angus arrived, his parents out on the balcony enjoying their breakfast and beach view in the morning sun.

"Angus, help yourself to pancakes, love," called Mrs McLeod, never missing an opportunity to ply him with food.

"Thanks, but I've eaten already," he called back.

Hamish listened with widening eyes as Angus filled him in on Leo.

"Crikey!" he said, "but wasn't he all set to win?"

"Yes. That's why it's so weird," said Angus. He told Hamish how no one else, including the police, was worried. Then he pulled out the napkin and explained where he'd found it.

"The Sea Shanty," read Hamish. "Where's that?"

"No idea. Can you Google it?"

Hamish fired up his laptop and in no time they established that The Sea Shanty was a seafood restaurant not too far away.

"A sumptuous selection of the finest seafood," read Hamish, "all locally sourced, open seven days, kids eat lunch free, Monday to Friday. Hey, sounds good. We should go."

"I *am* going," said Angus. "But not to eat the seafood."

"Why? You think it'll lead you to Leo?" Hamish sounded sceptical.

"I think it's worth a look. I'd really like to find out who dropped the napkin. But first I want to find out if Leo really has gone up to his parents' cabin on Mount Tamborine. To rule it out."

"Today?"

"Maybe. Or tomorrow."

"How are you going to get up there?"

"I don't know. Catch a bus I suppose. Wanna come?"

Hamish made a face and together they turned to look at his parents on the balcony. Hamish was not allowed to catch buses without either his mum or dad. There was no point even asking.

Hamish said, "I have to go shopping this morning, anyway. For new boardies. Sorry."

***

Angus jogged back toward the beach house. The wind had picked up further and his bare legs were stung by swirling sand. It was hard going jogging straight into it. The big outdoor umbrellas at the Italian café were rocking about in their bases. Ahead of Angus a mother pushed a baby in a carriage. As she passed the café, a fierce gust of wind lifted one of the umbrellas. It teetered in the air. It was going to topple over right on top of the mother and baby.

"Hey, look out!" Angus shouted, lunging to catch the umbrella. He grabbed its pole and managed to steady it just as the mother ducked out of the way with her baby. A near miss.

The grey-haired man ran from inside the café. "Oh-a my goodness! Are you all right, madam? I'm-a so sorry!" The lady assured him that she and her baby were just fine, thanks to Angus's quick thinking. She thanked him and walked on with the baby cooing happily.

"You are a good-a boy. Thank you, thank you. If that umbrella had-a hit that lady...? Oh dear-a me!" Angus helped him to right the umbrella and then held it while the man fetched extra sandbags to sit on all of the umbrella bases.

When they'd finished the man thanked him again and held out his hand.

"My name is Gianni Mancini. And you are...?"

"Angus. Angus Adams." He shook Mr Mancini's hand.

"Pleased to meet you, Angus," said the older man, smiling. "You are here on a holiday, yes? I see you and your friends going to beach, every day. Very good. Or maybe you are, how you say, a professional surfer, here for the big event, no?" Mr Mancini was teasing him.

"No," Angus said, laughing. "I'm only just learning how to surf. I don't even own my own board."

"Oh-a! Why you no have your own board?" Angus told him that even second-hand boards were expensive, but he was trying to save up for one, even though it was slow going.

"I can-a help you," said Mr Mancini. "I need someone to wash and polish all of my glasses," he waved a hand back at the café. "You come, in the mornings, early, seven o'clock and do my glasses for me and set up the tables and umbrellas. Yes? One hour. I pay you twenty dollars every day. Wadda you say?"

Wow. A real job. Awesome.

He said, "Thanks, if you're sure. I'm only staying for a few more days, though."

"No worries." Mr Mancini beamed. "Angus, I see you tomorrow!"

5 HOWAT!

At the beach house, Angus told Bodhi what he'd discovered about The Sea Shanty, which wasn't much. Bodhi reported that Leo hadn't been in touch. In general, the mood at the house was glum. Nate, who'd normally have been surfing for a couple hours, was out the back waxing his board. His face was downcast.

"You okay, Nate? How come you're not in the water yet?"

Nate looked up as he waxed. "Can't in this wind. Surf's blown out." Then he added, "I just don't get it, man. Why would he take off like that and not even tell me?"

"I don't know," said Angus. "He might come back."

"I kinda thought we were in this thing together, you know? Our first big title competition. We've been buddies for so long. I just don't get why he didn't talk to me first."

"What time is your dad getting here?" asked Angus. Reminding Nate that his father was flying in all the way from the US today might cheer him up.

"Soon, I hope," said Nate, looking back at his board.

Angus wanted to ask him about Leo's cabin. Find out exactly where on the mountain it was. But before he could, a television news van pulled into the driveway behind Mr Taylor's car. Angus watched as a well-groomed lady got out along with a guy holding a camera.

"Good morning," called the lady, now trying to hold her hair in place in the wind. "We understand that Leo Manning, pro surfer, has withdrawn from the Quick Silver event. We were hoping to get a statement?"

Mr Taylor came swiftly from the house.

"I'm sorry, we've no statement to make, thank you."

"If we could just speak with Mr Manning?" the lady reporter persisted.

"He's not here at present, thank you," Mr Taylor said.

"Can you confirm his whereabouts for us, then?"

At that moment Bodhi leaned over the deck and called, "Dad, there's a guy from a radio station on the phone asking about Leo."

Mr Taylor held up his hands. To the lady reporter he said, "We have no comment to make, other than Leo is not here at present. Thank you. Please remove your van from my driveway." Mr Taylor went inside. The news people hesitated but left when neither Nate nor Angus would speak to them either.

"Word travels fast," said Nate.

No sooner had the news crew left than another car pulled into the driveway. A tall, broad-shouldered man in a business suit got out. Nate's face lit up.

"Hey, Dad!" he said. The man held his arms

open wide to Nate and the two of them hugged.

When they separated, Nate did the introductions.

"Pleasure to meet you, young man." Mr Parker pumped Angus's hand with a firm grip and a smile. "You'll have to excuse my appearance, just came from the airport. Sixteen hours straight from LA. I'm jet-lagged as heck," he said, laughing and running a hand through his hair.

The mood in the house lifted with the arrival of Nate's dad. Nate was obviously delighted to see him and he was also an old friend of Bodhi's dad. He was super-thrilled, he said, that business had brought him out here and he'd be able to watch Nate surf in the competition on the weekend. His big, cheery personality was just what the house needed.

He listened in surprise to the tale of Leo's sudden departure but agreed with Mr Taylor that as Leo was legally an adult, there was no cause for immediate concern, he'd turn up in his own time, hopefully to compete, but if not then that was his choice.

"Now, I have a business meeting this afternoon, but first," he said, taking off his tie and laying it over the back of the chair, "I want to have a go at this game you all call cricket. I know nothing about it other than it involves using a bat to hit a ball and that you Aussies love it. Can't be that different from baseball, can it?"

Mr Taylor laughed. "Yes, it can," he said, "but I'm game. You guys up for some beach cricket?"

"Count me in," said Nate. He'd played a few games this week already and thought cricket was a blast.

Angus looked at Bodhi then said, "Ah, could you just give us a second?" and he pulled Bodhi into the kitchen. "I really wanted to show that circle and leaf drawing around and see if it means anything," he said.

"Well," said Bodhi, "I still think it looks Hawaiian and there're lots of Hawaiians competing this weekend. There might be some down on the beach. We could take it with us."

Angus thought about this. "Okay, sure. Tell your dad I'm in."

Onto a piece of paper, Angus carefully copied the circle and leaf doodle which had appeared on Leo's portfolio. It looked too stylised to be a random doodle. And the more he thought about it, the more he agreed with Bodhi that it could be Hawaiian. He put it into his pocket and then helped the others collect the cricket gear.

***

On the beach out the front of the surf club, Mr Taylor said, "It's a bit breezy, but we'll see how we go. Angus, bang in the wickets up there a bit, would you, mate? I'll put the other set here."

Angus used his bat to knock the stumps into the sand as Mr Taylor did his best to explain the basic rules of cricket to Mr Parker.

"Okay, so those stick things Angus is knocking into the sand are called the stumps or the wickets. The batsmen score runs by sprinting between the two sets of wickets. The fielding team bowl the ball overarm at the batsman and try to get him or her out by hitting the stumps and knocking off the bails."

"The bails?" asked Mr Parker, scratching his head.

"Those smaller stick things Angus is balancing on top of the stumps. Try to keep up, mate," Mr Taylor teased his friend.

"If you had any sense you'd just play baseball, like the rest of the world," said Mr Parker, with a twinkle in his eye.

Nate piped up, "Actually, Dad, cricket is the world's second biggest sport and has four times as many fans as baseball."

"Is that so?" said Mr Parker.

"Thank you, Nate. Both good points," said Mr Taylor. "Now, with beach or backyard cricket one person bats and everyone else fields. The batsman can be bowled out, or as in baseball, caught or run out. Normally the game's played on an oval four times the size of a baseball pitch. If you hit the ball to the boundary, it's a bonus and you score four runs, over the boundary on the full gets you six. Clear as mud?"

"Just about," said Mr Parker. "Time you stopped yakkin' and started playin'. Hand me the bat. I'm hitting me a six."

Angus handed the bat to Mr Parker and said, "On the beach, getting to the water's a four. Do it on the full and we'll give you six."

Mr Parker stood in front of the wicket and raised his bat up like he was playing baseball.

Bodhi laughed and said, "No, in cricket you hold the bat down like this."

"You know what," said Mr Parker, "why don't

you bat first so I can see how it's done."

"Good idea," said Bodhi, taking the bat.

Angus bowled six balls and Bodhi smashed each one to the water, nearly taking out a startled seagull with one shot. There were few sports she wasn't great at. Nate caught her out on the seventh ball to the cheers and claps from the others.

"I had the sun in my eyes," she said.

Nate took strike next. "Okay, let me have it," he called to Mr Taylor who was now bowling. And he did. The ball rocketed down toward Nate. He lifted his bat to strike but overshot it and the ball skipped under the bat to hit the middle stump, plumb on. It was knocked clean out of the sand, the bails flying.

"HOWZAT!" Mr Taylor screamed, throwing his arms up and out.

"How's *what*?" asked a bewildered Mr Parker.

"That's called appealing to the umpire," explained Angus, laughing at Mr Taylor's enthusiasm. "It means 'how's that?' like, is that good enough to be out?"

"But we don't have an umpire," said Mr Parker, still looking confused, "And he's clearly out, right, with those bail doo-hickeys flying in the air?"

"Yes," said Mr Taylor, "but it's fun to yell it

anyway."

They talked Mr Parker into having the next bat. Now holding it correctly, he faced Angus's ball and got a nice ground shot away.

"Run!" Bodhi yelled. Mr Parker took off across the sand and made a run before Nate got to the ball and threw it back. He hit the next ball to the water for four.

"Why didn't you tell me cricket was so easy?" he joked.

"Beginner's luck," said Mr Taylor. "Don't get comfortable. I bet you don't last another six balls."

"You're on. In fact, if I get out before then I'll take everyone out to dinner tonight. How's that sound?"

"Great. But you should know I'm planning on being very hungry," said Mr Taylor.

Mr Parker made runs on all of the next five balls. He really was pretty good with the bat.

"Looks like I get to save my money, tonight," Mr Parker said as Angus walked back for the final ball.

"Come on, Angus, we're counting on you," said Mr Taylor.

Angus ran in, swung his right arm back and over, tucked the left one in tight, and let the ball go.

It flew down the sandy pitch straight as an arrow, under Mr Parker's mistimed strike to hit him square on the left leg and bounce away.

"HOWZAT?" Angus yelled, jumping up and down.

"OUT!" called Mr Taylor. Nate ran in to high five everyone.

"What? What out?" said Mr Parker looking around at the wicket in confusion. "How is that out? It didn't touch the wicket."

"LBW, mate," said Mr Taylor. "Leg Before Wicket. You can't stop the ball hitting the wicket by putting your leg in the way."

"You didn't tell me that before."

"You sure?" said Mr Taylor.

"Yes, old friend, I'm sure," said Mr Parker pretending to look cross. Then he grinned. "But, tell you what. Playing cricket's been a real hoot. I'm gonna take you all out for dinner anyway!"

Mr Parker had to get to his meeting so the game was declared over and the others headed back, leaving Angus and Bodhi on the beach.

"Come on," said Angus, "Let's show the drawing to some of those surfers over there on the rocks."

6 THE KORU

It was a good thing the wind was up. It meant a lot of the surfers were on the beach or the rocks rather than out in the water. They showed the drawing to a few of them without success. No one knew what it might mean, if it actually meant anything at all.

Angus was almost ready to give up when Bodhi pointed out Keanu Hale, one of the pro surfers, talking to a reporter on the boardwalk.

"He's Hawaiian, at least," she said.

"Will he talk to us?" Angus said.

"Let's find out," said Bodhi.

When the reporter left, they approached Hale and asked politely if he recognised the image. He considered it. "Koru," he said. "A fern leaf. Means 'new life'. Not sure about the circle."

"Thanks!" said Angus

"Happy to help," said Hale and moved away to sign autographs for a gaggle of teenage girls.

To Bodhi, Angus said, "Well, it's a start."

"I guess," she said. "But, I can't see how it helps much."

***

On the way back to the beach house they passed the surf club.

"Hey, look at that," said Bodhi, pointing at a notice pinned to the surf club wall. It read:

Kids' Pizza-Making Competition

Thursday Night 6.30pm

Best Pizza wins a Brand New Firewire Surfboard!

"You make great pizza," said Bodhi. "You should totally enter."

Angus thought about this. At home, he had to do

his share of the family cooking. It was something he enjoyed but he'd never entered any type of competition before.

"You think?" he said.

"Sure. Why not?"

It *would* be pretty cool to win the surfboard. It would mean not having to spend his café earnings on one. He shrugged, and added his name to the entrants' list.

***

That evening, true to his word, Mr Parker took everyone to dinner at a very fancy restaurant on the top floor of the very fancy hotel where he was staying. Angus, wearing his one and only pair of fancy pants, and being a bit of a cook himself, enjoyed seeing the culinary creations the fine dining chefs produced. Even if he was just a little scared he would use the wrong fork.

"I wonder if The Sea Shanty is anything like this?" he half-joked to Bodhi. Mr Parker overheard him.

"The Sea Shanty? That sounds interesting. What is it?" he asked. Before Angus could answer, Mr Taylor started telling him about the napkin Angus had found and his theory that there might be more to Leo's disappearance than everyone thought.

Angus reddened. The whole idea sounded stupid, spelt out like that. Mr Parker would think he was an idiot. Which was more or less confirmed when he laughed and said, "So we have a young detective in our midst? Good for you, young man. Keep us all up-to-date on what you discover, won't you?" Angus felt like a silly little kid.

But then Mr Taylor said, "Leo still hasn't returned my call. I've been thinking that Angus does have a point about the cabin up on Tamborine Mountain. I'm thinking it might not be a bad idea to head up there tomorrow and just see if he *is* there. Just to check he's okay. You kids can come with me, if you like."

**

Angus was up early the next morning. He had to be at his new job by seven and they were leaving at nine for the drive up the mountain. At ten to seven, he crossed the road to Rosa's Italian Café. It was a fine day, with no wind.

"Nice and early! I like-a that," said Mr Mancini. "You are good boy, Angus. Come, come, I show you inside." There were more tables inside and Angus helped Mr Mancini take down the chairs.

"Who's Rosa?" Angus asked, keen to learn how the café got its name. Mr Mancini stopped and put his hand on his heart.

"Oh, my beautiful Rosa. She was-a my wife." He made the sign of the cross; he touched his forehead, his chest, then his left and right shoulders. "Such a wonderful lady, you don't know. I still miss her so much."

"I'm sorry," said Angus, worried that he'd upset the older man.

"No, no, don't be sorry," Mr Mancini said quickly. "She gone very long time, now. I have four beautiful daughters and many grandchildren. Look, look." He took out his wallet and showed Angus photos of happy smiling kids and plump babies. The last photo was an old black-and-white of a smiling bride.

"That's my Rosa," said Mr Mancini.

"She *was* beautiful," said Angus.

"You good boy," said Mr Mancini, smiling. Then he showed Angus the small dishwasher behind the counter used for glasses and how to work it. Angus washed and polished all the glassware then helped set up the outdoor tables and umbrellas, making sure each was secured with a couple of sandbags around the base.

At eight o'clock, Mr Mancini gave Angus a twenty dollar note.

"You do good job. I hope you come back tomorrow," he said.

Angus grinned. "For sure," he said, putting the money in his pocket. "Thanks, Mr Mancini. I'll see you tomorrow."

He ran across the street to the beach house, eager to get going up the mountain. Mr Taylor stood in the driveway looking down at the car. He looked up at Angus.

"Sorry, mate. We're not going anywhere today," he said.

7 THREE DAYS TO GO

"**W**hy not?" Angus asked. Then he saw. The car was sitting weirdly low. All four tyres were flat. They'd been slashed. *What?*

"You're kidding? When? Who?"

"Sometime last night. Kids with nothing better to do, probably," said Mr Taylor.

This was unbelievable. How could anyone do that? Okay, definitely not going up the mountain in the car, then.

There wasn't really much Angus could do to help. Mr Taylor had arranged for new tyres but it would be late afternoon before the car was good to go. He didn't want to wait until tomorrow. He'd take the bus instead. There was no point in asking Hamish to come. He asked Bodhi but she wanted to spend the day with her father. Angus understood. Bodhi didn't see her dad very often. He lived in Sydney while she and her brother lived with their mother in Brisbane. They had to make the most of their holiday together.

***

The bus rattled along. Through the window, Angus watched as steel and glass high-rises gave way to the red and brown rooftops of suburbia. Soon, even the houses thinned out and they passed through the farmland that footed the mountain. A couple of kangaroos, spooked by the bus, bounded away across a paddock, through the sheep and into bushland.

Moving down through its gears, the bus began slowly climbing the winding mountain road. If the window had been the type that opened Angus could have reached out and touched the gumtrees.

He'd been lucky to get his seat up the back. The

bus was almost full with day-tripping tourists. On the Gold Coast, Mount Tamborine was nearly as big an attraction as the beach, with its arts and craft shops, weekend markets, country cafés and cabins.

Eventually they entered the village and the bus shuddered to a stop. The tourists disembarked, meandering away, cameras around their necks. Angus studied the directions Nate had given him. Okay, left at the post-office, then a right two blocks later into Mulberry Lane.

Three minutes later he was standing out the front of a small log cabin. It had been built into the side of the mountain, supported by long steel poles. Number 16. This was it. The driveway was empty but a white van sat on the street nearby. No neighbours to speak of. Just another couple of cabins up the road a bit.

Suddenly Angus felt silly, certain now that Leo would be here and possibly resent the intrusion. He began mentally rehearsing what he might say; something about being up here anyway so thought he might as well pop in and say hi?

Whatever. Just get on with it. He climbed the front steps to the veranda noticing the closed windows on a warm day. The veranda ran around the side of the cabin and Angus followed it searching for a front door. Or a back door. Any door would do. He finally found one and stopped in surprise.

The door was open. So Leo *was* here. Rapping on the open door, he called out, "Leo?"

There were dull thumping noises coming from inside. From the doorway he could see an empty sitting room.

"Leo, you there? It's me, Angus."

The thumping noises stopped. Silence. Now what? Go on in? Leave? No, he'd spent half the morning getting here. He wasn't leaving until he knew if Leo was okay.

"Leo, I'm coming in," he called. He pushed the door wider and walked through to the living room.

Suddenly, a person rushed at him from a doorway on the other side of the room, nearly knocking him over, not to mention frightening the life out of him. It wasn't Leo.

"You again! Waddya doing here, kid?" Angus stared in surprise.

It was Dylan.

Dylan, the surfer jerk. And he had a surfboard under his arm. A Forget Me Not.

"Isn't that Leo's board?" Angus didn't know what was going on but he wasn't going to let Dylan the jerk just walk out with Leo's board.

"None of your business. Now get out of the way." Then he added, "Leo said I could borrow it." It was a lie. Angus was sure of it. Dylan went to push past but Angus stood in his way.

"Is Leo here, then?"

"I told you to get out of my way!" He shoved Angus in the chest. He fell back against the wall. Dylan strode out the door with the board. At the window, Angus watched him toss it into the back of the van on the street, then drive off. In a hurry.

He looked around the cabin quickly. It felt wrong to be in Leo's place without him but he wanted to check for signs someone was staying here. The two small bedrooms off the sitting room contained only neatly-made beds. No bags or clothes lying around. The bathroom was empty of towels or toiletries. The fridge was also empty and switched off, the door open. No food in the kitchen cupboards.

There was no one staying here. Time to go. He pulled the door shut on his way out.

He was walking up the driveway when another

vehicle pulled up out the front. It was Mr Parker, Nate's dad, in his silver rental. He got out of the car. He was again wearing a business suit. "Angus, hey! I heard about the car. Too bad, right?"

"The tyres? Yeah," Angus said. What was Mr Parker doing here?

The man glanced at the cabin then back at Angus. "Nate told me you'd bussed it up here and since I was coming up on business anyway, thought I'd see if you want a lift back?"

Oh. Sure. Why not? It would be quicker than taking the bus.

"Thanks. That'd be great," he said.

"That is, if you can trust a Yank to stick to the left side of the road," Mr Parker said, laughing. He moved a bag of what looked like groceries from the front seat so that Angus could sit down.

"So, any sign of Leo?" Mr Parker asked, pulling away from the curb.

"No. I'm sure he's not here," said Angus. He told Mr Parker about Dylan storming out with the surfboard.

"Interesting," he said. "Don't know the boy, myself, but I've heard he's not the friendliest guy around. Do you think he broke in to steal Leo's board?"

"I couldn't see how he got in. The door didn't look damaged. But yeah, I think he was stealing the board. Probably thinks it'll help him win."

"Well, I guess there's not a whole lot we can do about it until Leo shows up. Can't prove Leo didn't say he could take the board." They drove in silence for a while.

Then Mr Parker said, "I have to say I admire your initiative, young man. But do your parents worry about you catching buses all alone?"

"No. They know I'm sensible and they trust me to make smart choices," said Angus. This made Mr Parker chuckle.

"Good for them. And I agree. It's good for kids to be independent." Mr Parker glanced out the window at the view from the mountain all the way to the ocean. "Wow. Look at that. This sure is a beautiful part of the world, Angus. I wish I was here for a vacation. But, you know what they say, no rest for the weary."

Mr Parker let Angus out at the beach house

"Here, take these," he said. He took something out of his pocket and held them out through the window. It was three tickets to 'Around The World

Putt Putt'. A mini golf place up the coast a bit.

"Awesome. Thanks!" said Angus taking the tickets.

"No worries, as you Aussies say," Mr Parker said, chuckling. "A client gave them to me but I can't use them. Don't let this whole thing with Leo ruin your school vacation. Take young Bodhi and someone else, if you like, and have some fun."

8 FRECKLES, CURLY, & THE TOAD

"**A** *job*, Angus?" Mrs McLeod was navigating her way along the highway to the mini-golf place for an evening of fun. Angus, Bodhi, and Hamish were all in the back. "Have you checked to make sure your parents are okay with that? I mean, I don't think it's legal to hire children." She glanced at him in the rear-view mirror with a furrowed brow.

"Mu-um," Hamish said, rolling his eyes. "He's just washing a few glasses for an hour a day. It's not like he's chained to a sewing machine in a third-world factory stitching tee shirts. It's not fair. I wish *I* had a job."

"Well that won't be happening any time soon, lad," said Mrs McLeod.

Angus said, "I haven't actually told my parents yet, but you're right, Mrs McLeod, I should definitely do that. I'm due to call them tomorrow, anyway." Mrs McLeod seemed happy enough with this answer. You had to know how to talk to adults.

"Right-o, here we are," Mrs McLeod sang, pulling into a carpark. Angus peered out the window.

"AROUND THE WORLD MINI GOLF – WHERE THE FUN NEVER STOPS" screamed the huge sign perched above a rotating world globe. "Open 7 days 10am to 10pm" was in smaller print underneath.

"False advertising," said Bodhi. Angus raised his eyebrows. "Well, clearly the fun stops for a good twelve hours every day." Trust Bodhi to notice that.

As they climbed from the car, Hamish nudged Angus.

"Look who's here," he said quietly, looking toward the queue of people at the entrance.

"Oh, no," said Angus. Up the front of the queue was Rapata Takani, Angus's arch enemy from school. "What's *he* doing here?"

"Lots of people holiday on the coast, Angus," said Bodhi.

In prep, Rapata had taken an inexplicable dislike to Angus and from then on never missed an opportunity to cause trouble for him in any way he could. Over the years, Angus found that ignoring him, or even better, just staying out of his way, was the best strategy. Rapata was twice as tall and broad as most other kids their age so he wasn't someone you wanted to pick a fight with if it could be avoided. Unfortunately, Angus hadn't been able to avoid it last term when he'd accidently knocked out one of Rapata's teeth during a soccer game. Rapata had tried to extract revenge with his fists and ended up suspended from school as a result. He would not have forgotten.

"Should be okay," said Bodhi. "He's way ahead of us in the queue. There'll be a few groups of people playing between him and us."

"Sure," said Angus.

After some time, they made it to the front of the queue, received their score cards and putters and

57

waited for their turn to tee off. Mrs McLeod sat herself down in the eating area, overlooking the course, with a tall mug of coffee and a magazine.

The Grand Canyon was up first. You had to putt your ball over a series of narrow bridges crossing the 'canyon'. Bodhi won, sinking her ball in three putts to Angus and Hamish's five. This was no surprise as there wasn't much Bodhi *wasn't* good at. She could outswim them, out soccer them, and out Karate them. So *of course* she could out putt them. In other people, this might have been annoying but Bodhi was generally so quiet and humble about her natural abilities that you ended up just liking her more.

The next hole was the Eiffel Tower. Bodhi putted skilfully around a couple of mounds, set herself up beautifully to go straight under the tower and then did so, putting her ball into the hole for a total of four shots. Angus fumbled his way around the mounds, eventually made it under the tower and then into the hole for six. Poor Hamish had a shocker. He just couldn't get past the first mound, claimed the hole was rigged, and then hit the ball too hard in his frustration and knocked it right out of the course. He finished the hole with a nine and a red face.

The Egyptian Pyramids were next. Bodhi putted her ball neatly through the tunnel under the first pyramid. Angus did the same. Both balls appeared on the other side. Hamish gave a loud, "Yes!" when his ball, too, went neatly into the first pyramid. But the joy was short-lived. Hamish's ball did not appear out the other side.

"Huh? Where is it?" he said, on his knees trying to peer into the tunnel. "Too dark. Can't see a thing." He reached his hand into the tunnel.

"Ugh...there's something squishy blocking the tunnel. If I can just..." His face twisted with effort. He pulled out his arm.

"Crikey!" Clutched in his fist was a fat cane toad.

Bodhi gave a little scream and jumped back. "Yuck," she said, wrinkling her nose. Angus couldn't help but jump back also, just managing not to scream himself. Hamish laughed.

"Crikey, you should see your faces. It's just a cane toad. There you go, feller." He carefully put the toad down in the leafy garden. "There are lots of them about now that the weather's warmer."

"They're poisonous," said Bodhi, still pulling a face. "I had a dog once that died after biting a cane toad."

"The key word in that sentence is 'biting'. Don't try to eat one and you'll be okay," said Hamish, the expert on all wildlife matters. "Still, I'll just wash my hands before we play on."

They finished the hole with Bodhi scoring three to Angus and Hamish's four each. They rounded a corner to start the next hole but the group in front of them were still on it. It was a father with two young boys, one very freckly, the other with tight, curly hair. As the father went to make his putt, a cane toad jumped from the garden onto the course, landing smack over the hole.

"Get out of here, you mongrel!" he said, and lifted his putter into the air over his shoulder. He was going to take a swing at the cane toad.

"Hey!" Hamish called out and rushed forward. "Don't do that, you'll hurt it!" Hamish would never stand by and allow any animal, even a cane toad, to be hurt.

The father looked up, clearly annoyed. "They're pests, should be killed, the lot of them."

"You don't have to be cruel, though," argued Hamish.

"Kill it, Dad!" called Freckles.

"Yeah, smash its guts everywhere," yelled Curly. The father took aim again. To Hamish he said, "Get lost, kid."

"Wait, let me catch it," said Hamish and he made a dash at the toad. The sudden movement startled it and it jumped to the next hole. Hamish, the man, Freckles and Curly all looked at each other.

And then it was on.

Freckles and Curly chased the toad onto the next hole, clubs raised and shouting, "Kill it, kill it!"

Hamish took off after them, yelling, "Stop! Stop!"

Angus and Bodhi looked at each other then joined in the chase, the father bringing up the rear, waving his putter about wildly and yelling something about idiot kids.

The toad led them all on a merry chase as people either moved out of the way to watch or joined in. Curly got close on the Sydney Harbour Bridge, took a swipe and missed, in the process nearly whacking an elderly lady in the face. On the Great Wall of China, Hamish overtook Freckles and Curly to take the lead. The toad jumped onto the Tower of London and Hamish almost had it but tripped over his own feet and fell like a sack of potatoes. At this point Angus and Bodhi took up the charge, leaping over Hamish's body, for the three of them were nothing if not a team.

Angus gained on the toad, Bodhi hot on his heels and the two sons still behind, shouting and waving their putters in the air. The toad leapt into the Niagara Falls, probably hoping to find refuge in the water. At last, it was cornered. All Angus had to do was scoop it up.

He reached down. "Come on, mate," he said. But Freckles was having none of it and shoved Angus viciously in the back, shouting, "Death to the toad!" Angus fell on his knees into the water. Freckles swiped and missed. The toad leapt for its life, out of the Falls and straight onto a table in the dining area, amidst the horrified diners.

Rapata Takani stared at his pizza, his brain trying to process why a fat cane toad was now stuck in the mozzarella and pepperoni. Slowly his expression changed from bewildered to angry. He looked up and made eye contact with Angus, stunned and dripping wet before him. As recognition took hold his face went from angry to murderous. Angus's first instinct was to bolt. But Rapata could hardly beat him to a pulp here in front of everyone, surely. No, he'd save it for back at school.

Great.

"Adams," Rapata said. Then he lifted his enormous hand and, staring Angus in the eyes, slowly drew a finger across his neck.

9 TWO DAYS TO GO

It was another glorious morning. The sunshine was warm and a light breeze tickled the back of his neck as Angus pushed the broom across the al fresco area of Rosa's Italian Café. So far this morning, he'd polished all the glasses and cutlery and taken down the chairs from the indoor tables. All that remained was to set up the outdoor tables and umbrellas.

As he swept, three surfers with boards under their arms walked over to him.

"Any chance of a coffee, mate?" one of them asked.

"Uh, I'm not sure if we're open yet. I'll just get the owner." Angus called out to Mr Mancini who came bustling out, wiping his hands on a tea-towel.

"Yes, yes, boys," he said to the surfers with his usual big friendly smile. "We not officially open until ten but for you, I do coffee. Come, come, Angus help me with a table." Angus helped him to carry out a table and set up the umbrella.

"Thanks, much appreciated, Sir," said another of the surfers with an American accent. In no time, Mr Mancini had made them all extra-large cappuccinos. Angus got on with his work setting up the rest of the outdoor tables. When he was done, Mr Mancini gave him twenty dollars and a large plastic container filled with handmade pasta.

"Left over spaghetti from-a last night. You and your friends enjoy."

"Thank you," Angus said, thinking this was perfect as he was rostered to cook everyone dinner tonight.

"No, no, thank *you*, Angus. You are good boy. I wish you work for me all the time. Now go. It beautiful day. Go and have fun."

Angus walked past the three surfers who were still finishing their coffees. On an impulse, he turned back to them. "Excuse me," he said, "but I was wondering if any of you know what this symbol means?" From his pocket he took his sketch of the drawing that had been left on Leo's portfolio. "I've been told the leaf's Hawaiian but I'm not sure if the circle means anything."

The surfers each looked at the sketch but none could tell Angus anymore about it.

"You know who might know?" said the American. "Mr Kahue. Old Hawaiian dude. Makes surf boards here in Rainbow Bay."

"Really?" said Angus. "Where exactly?" The surfer told him the name of the street.

"Old house next to the bakery. You'll find him round back."

Angus hurried across the road to tell Bodhi.

***

He found her in the kitchen, stacking the dishwasher with breakfast dishes. Angus put his container of spaghetti into the refrigerator then began rinsing cereal bowls and handing them to her for stacking in the washer.

"Kahue. Yeah, I think I've heard Taj mention

him," said Bodhi. "Makes awesome boards, but is supposed to be a bit weird."

"Weird how?" asked Angus.

"Not sure, exactly. I'm coming with you."

***

It was an easy ten minute walk away, just the other side of Point Danger.

"Point Danger. Dramatic sounding name, isn't it?" said Angus, gazing up at the rocky headland. "I wonder why it's called that."

"It was named by Captain Cook in 1770," said Bodhi. "No one really knows why." Trust Bodhi to know that. "It's right next to Snapper Rocks so maybe he thought the rocks were dangerous. You know, for ships or whatever." Angus hoped the 'danger' part wasn't going to be a bad omen for Leo.

Things were pretty quiet when they found the street. It was off the beaten track a bit, with no flashy restaurants or cafés, so no reason for the tourists to come into it. They spotted the bakery quickly enough. On its far side was a run-down looking house. The picket fence was missing pickets and the patch of lawn in the front yard was overgrown. The place looked abandoned.

"Do you think this is it?" said Bodhi, peering at

the closed windows on the house.

"Must be. They said it was next to the bakery and there's nothing else here that could be it. Anyway we're supposed to find him round the back." They both looked at the concrete drive running down the side of the house.

"Come on," said Angus.

Halfway down the drive, they heard noise. It was some sort of electric tool thrumming away. They rounded the back corner of the house and found themselves in a large yard. It held a big open shed adorned with surfboards in all stages of production. Some wood, some foam. Out in the middle of the yard, in the open air, a board had been placed on a wooden workhorse. Bent over it was a tiny old man. He was running an electric planer over the board. The man wasn't just old. He was ancient. At least ninety, thought Angus. And that was being generous.

For a few minutes they stood and watched the man shape the board. He didn't seem to notice them and Angus wasn't sure how to proceed. He looked at Bodhi. She shrugged.

A large, fluffy grey Persian cat strolled leisurely out of the shed. It looked at the two of them before ambling over and lovingly rubbing itself first against Bodhi's bare legs and then Angus. Bodhi bent and patted its head. It looked up at her and purred.

Suddenly, all was quiet as the planing stopped. The man was still bent over the board.

"Ah...excuse me?" Angus said.

Without looking up, the old man shot one hand out in the 'stop' sign at Angus.

"Don't speak!" he snapped. Angus jumped and almost bit his tongue. Without taking his eyes from the board, the old man put the planer down on the bench beside him, picked up what looked like a small piece of steel mesh, and began rubbing it across the nose of the board.

"Have to get this just right. Yes...yes...almost...nearly there...yes!" He stood back from the board admiring his work and then, finally looked at Angus and Bodhi. His face broke into a smile, pulling all the wrinkles up around twinkling eyes. "Sorry. Have to concentrate when I'm doing the tricky bits. How can I help you? You need a surfboard? I have lots of surfboards." He waved his arm at the shed full of boards.

Angus said, "Ah, no, I–"

"You sure? You are short, true," he said, looking Angus up and down, "but still I can make you a wonderful board." Then he looked at Bodhi. "Or perhaps the board is for the young lady. You are very graceful, Miss, if you don't mind me saying so. You hold yourself straight. Very strong. You would make a wonderful surfer."

Angus immediately straightened his own shoulders. Bodhi laughed. "Are you Mr Kahue?" she said.

"At your service, Miss." The little man bowed his head.

"Your surfboards look wonderful but, actually, we were hoping you could give us some information."

"Is that so?" He bent to pat the cat that was now rubbing against him. "What information could I possibly have for you?"

Bodhi nudged Angus. "Um, could you please have a look at this?" he said, and fumbled in his pocket before bringing out the sketch and clumsily unfolding it. He gave it to Mr Kahue. "It's supposed to be Hawaiian and so we thought you might know what it means."

"Hang on, need my reading glasses." They

waited as Mr Kahue hunted about for his glasses until Bodhi pointed out that they were hanging around his neck.

"Oh, yes, silly me," he said. Once he had his glasses on, the old man peered at the sketch. "Ah, Koru. That's the fern leaf. Means new beginnings, or new life, if you will."

"Yes, we've been told that," said Angus, "but we're wondering if the circle around it means anything."

"Yes. Clever boy," said Mr Kahue. "Princess Lydia was right about you." *Huh? Princess Lydia?* Angus and Bodhi looked at each other. Mr Kahue continued,

"The circle represents continuity." He handed the sketch back to Angus. "Put simply, a circle around the Koru means 'circle of life'."

"Circle of life. Okay, thanks very much, Mr Kahue," said Angus, putting the sketch back in his pocket and wondering if that helped at all.

"Be careful, won't you," the old man said, not smiling now.

"Um," said Angus, glancing at Bodhi, "I, er..." He wasn't sure what to say. Why was this strange little man telling him to be careful? They'd said nothing

71

of their mission to find Leo.

"Princess Lydia says you are in grave danger, young man. She says you are very intelligent but still you must take care. Three times soon you will be in big danger. Three times." He held up three fingers as he said this.

This was getting awkward. Bodhi spoke up,

"Mr Kahue, who is Princess Lydia?"

The old man threw his head back and laughed. He picked up the cat. "This is my beautiful Princess Lydia. Sorry, I neglected to introduce you. You must think I'm a silly old man." The cat purred.

Bodhi and Angus exchanged a glance. Okay, so the guy thought his cat could talk.

"Her full name is Princess Lydia Liliuokalani Kawānanakoa." He stroked the cat and looked at Bodhi. "Princess Lydia says that you also were a Hawaiian princess. In a previous life, of course."

Of course. 'Cos otherwise that'd be weird. Angus tried not to laugh.

Bodhi beamed, clearly enjoying the idea of once being a princess.

"But you were thrown into a volcano. A sacrifice to the gods," Mr Kahue continued.

Bodhi's face fell. Angus laughed. Couldn't help

himself.

"No, no," said Mr Kahue. "Being hurled into a volcano is the highest of honours. You should be very proud."

"Okay," said Bodhi, scratching her head. "Tell Princess Lydia I am honoured."

Mr Kahue looked confused. "She's not deaf. She can hear you herself."

"Oh, of course. Sorry," Bodhi said quickly.

"Anyway," continued Mr Kahue, putting the cat down. "Back to you, young man. You need to pay heed to the warning. Big danger ahead for you. Here. Come." He turned to the shed and waved at them to follow.

Bodhi whispered to Angus, "I didn't think Hawaiians made human sacrifices. Wasn't it the Aztecs who threw people into volcanos?"

"I dare you to tell him," whispered back Angus. Bodhi stuck out her tongue.

The old Hawaiian led them over to a workbench and pulled out a drawer. It looked to be packed with an assortment of odds and ends. Mr Kahue rummaged around in it.

"I'm sure there's one in here somewhere...yes, here it is!" He pulled out a necklace of some kind and held it up. It looked like a wooden fish hook attached to a leather string. He held it out to Angus.

"Makau. Fish hook. The ancestors used the fish hook to find food. Today it's a symbol of strength and prosperity. And most importantly for you, good luck. Wear it around your neck. It will help you to stay safe. You're in very grave danger, did I mention that?"

"Yes, you did," said Angus, taking the gift and fitting the string over his head. "Wow. Thanks very much." It *did* look pretty cool. He almost looked like a real surfer.

"And for you, young lady, the Honu." He pulled another necklace from the draw. This one had a little turtle attached to the leather string. "The green sea turtle. It brings good luck, endurance, and a long life. No volcanoes this time for you."

"It's beautiful. Thank you very much, Mr Kahue," said Bodhi, placing the turtle around her neck.

They said goodbye to the old man and his talking cat and walked back out to the street.

"Seriously, I'm pretty sure Hawaiians, as a rule, didn't throw people into volcanos," said Bodhi looking at her turtle.

"Let it go," said Angus.

"You're just jealous 'cos I was a Princess."

"Burnt to a crisp in a volcano. Anyway, the cat said I was intelligent. So there."

"Yeah, you're a regular Einstein. I'm hungry. Wanna get a pie from the bakery?" Angus did. Bodhi bought a steak and onion pie and Angus got a sausage roll. They walked up to the beach and sat on a bench to eat, watching the Pacific Ocean roll in.

"Okay, so the drawing means 'circle of life'," said Bodhi between bites. "So, what now?"

"I'm going to check out The Sea Shanty. That napkin is the only other clue we have. Time's running out for Leo. The competition's in two days. Wanna come, too?" said Angus, shaking pastry flakes from his tee shirt.

"Sorry, Dad wants me to go surfing with him this afternoon. Hey, do you think it's safe? To go by yourself, I mean. You know, with the whole grave danger, three times thing?"

Angus laughed. "I think I'll risk it."

10 DEATH WISH

If he'd had his bike with him, Angus could have ridden to The Sea Shanty in ten or fifteen minutes. As it was, he had to take the bus again.

He got off at a stop he hoped wasn't too far from the restaurant. His luck was in. Up the street, a large flashing neon sign, complete with a winking fish, announced it. Good thing Hamish wasn't there to see the winking.

He made his way along the footpath passing a

couple of surf shops and a McDonalds. Once at the restaurant, he stopped to look at it. There was a large veranda out the front covered with plastic tables and chairs, many still occupied by the late lunch crowd. Off the veranda was an indoor dining area and next to that, facing the street, was a take-away section that also sold fresh seafood.

Okay, now what?

He really hadn't thought that far ahead. He'd hoped that seeing the restaurant might lead to another clue as to where Leo might be.

A teenage waitress cleared tables on the veranda. Angus walked up the steps to her.

"Excuse me?" he said.

She looked up at him and scowled, clearly annoyed by the interruption. "Yes?"

"Um...I was just wondering if you could please tell me, um, do you know if Leo Manning has been in here recently?"

"Who?"

"Leo Manning. The pro surfer. He's competing in the Quick Silver Competition this weekend." The waitress's eyes widened.

"Oh, he's the one who's missing, right?"

"Yes."

She thought for a second before shaking her head. "Nope. Pretty sure he hasn't been in here. Why did you think he would have? And who are you?"

"Just a friend. One of your napkins was kind of found with his stuff, that's all."

She shrugged, bored now. "Sorry, kid, can't help you." She turned her back on him and headed to the kitchen.

Well, this was a big fat waste of time. Angus walked around the veranda to the take-away section. They had some nice-looking king prawns on ice. Shrimp, as Nate would say. He decided to buy some. Cooked up with garlic and lemon they'd be awesome with Mr Mancini's spaghetti. The prawns were expensive but he had his job money and some money his parents had given him for the week so, parting with his hard-earned cash, he tucked the paper package under his arm for the short walk back to the bus stop.

He turned.

And found himself staring into an enormous chest. He looked up. The chest had a head attached to it. The head and the chest belonged to Rapata Takani.

Not good.

"Hi, Rapata. I–"

"Adams." Rapata grabbed Angus's free arm with his huge hand. Out from behind Rapata came an even larger giant. A giant who looked a lot like Rapata. Older brother? He looked down at Angus. He wasn't smiling.

"Rapata, we can talk about this," tried Angus.

"You need to be taught a lesson, Adams," said Rapata. "And school's in." He pulled Angus down the steps, the brother right behind.

The bus was coming up the street.

But Rapata pulled him the other way. Angus resisted as best he could, but it was pointless. Rapata was strong. The brother loped along on his other side, still saying nothing. Maybe he couldn't talk.

"Rapata, don't be stupid," Angus tried again. "I know you're still angry about the accident at soccer last term, but it was an accident, I swear." He looked over his shoulder. The bus was indicating to pull into the stop.

"Why'd you throw that cane toad onto my pizza last night, Adams?"

"I didn't throw it. I was trying to catch it."

A lady got off the bus.

"Gotta a death wish, I reckon." Rapata and the brother both laughed.

"Yeah, death wish," said the brother. So he could talk.

Angus glanced back again desperately. Another lady was struggling to get on the bus with a baby carriage. It looked like the driver was helping her.

Angus's brain raced. Heaven knew where they were dragging him to. The lady and the carriage were now on the bus. Its doors were shutting.

He had one shot.

"POLICE! HELP!" he shouted.

The brother took his eyes off Angus to look around wildly for the police. Angus raised his right foot and stomped it down on Rapata's left one as hard as he could. Rapata cried out and let go. Angus whirled around and took off for the bus, his prawns still tucked under his arm.

"Wait!" he yelled, running for his life down the street, waving his free arm at the bus frantically. The brother, realising he'd been duped, pelted after him, Rapata limping and swearing along behind.

"Wait! Wait!" Angus shouted. But the bus driver either didn't hear him or didn't care. The bus pulled away from the curb.

With nothing else for it, Angus kept running. He glanced over his shoulder. The brother was gaining on him. Further up the street was the bridge leading over the wide Tweed River. Angus ran toward it. He tried to think but his brain wouldn't work. He needed a plan but nothing was coming. As he approached the bridge he could see it was for vehicles only. No pedestrian access. To his left the footpath lead away and down under the bridge but it was blocked off by some high temporary fencing. A sign said 'CLOSED FOR CONSTRUCTION WORK'.

He glanced over his shoulder. The brother was almost on him. He dropped the prawns and scaled the fence, half slipping down the other side, and scrambled down the path to go under the bridge. What? Oh, no. He could see now why the path was closed for construction. A five metre section of it had collapsed into the river. Where it was gone, the water lapped right up to the sheer retaining wall. Angus wasn't bad at long jump but five metres was ridiculous. He wasn't going to get through that way.

He looked back. The brother was climbing the fence. He looked the other way, frantically. A solid wall, eight feet high ran down the bank to the water. Total dead end. Rapata had reached the fence now, puffing hard. The brother was coming over the fence.

Angus looked at the river. The water was murky and running fast. Being just inland of the river mouth , the tide was coming in at a terrific pace.

The brother was halfway down the embankment. Angus looked back at the river. It was huge. He'd never be able to swim across it, trying would be suicide.

He leapt into the water.

11 DON'T THINK ABOUT SHARKS!

His only chance was to go with the current. Let the river carry him away and hope to get out somewhere upstream. At least the water wasn't cold. He looked back as he was swept away. The brother was at the river's edge staring after him. Rapata was still at the top of the embankment, behind the fence. He held something up. It was the package of king prawns. The *expensive* king prawns. He called out something which might have been, "Thanks!"

Angus was a confident swimmer, but this was terrifying. With the current incredibly strong, he concentrated on trying to relax and float. There was no point fighting it. Fighting would get him drowned. He told himself this was *fine*. Just like Bulcock Beach. Every Easter, his family camped at Caloundra, and swam at Bulcock Beach along the mouth of the river. All the kids had a ball jumping in and being swept along with the outgoing tide to wash up on the sand a bit further along, only to run back and do it again. It was *fun*. This was just the same. Okay, maybe not quite as much fun.

He tried desperately not to think about sharks. It was not unheard of for them to be seen in this river so close to the ocean. *Don't think about sharks, don't think about sharks, DO NOT THINK ABOUT SHARKS!*

He was swept upriver and eventually around a wide bend. Up ahead, some of the riverfront homes had their own private jetties. This could be his chance. As he neared the first one he tried to steer himself in toward it, hoping to grasp onto a support. It came at him. He stretched his arm out and...missed. It was just beyond his reach. He sailed right by it. The next one was coming up. Try again. The jetty rushed up at him. He tried to half-steer, half-swim himself toward it. This time he actually got an arm around the pole but it was as slippery as a wet fish. He couldn't get a grip. The water tore him away.

The current continued to carry him upriver. It was getting harder to stay calm and not fight it. Up ahead was another jetty. It had a large speedboat moored to it. Should he try it? What if he whacked straight into the boat? Would it kill him? He was heading straight for it. No steering required. For a second, he thought about trying to steer out *around* it but then something touched his foot.

A SHARK? He screamed like a little girl and made for the boat as though his life depended on it – which it probably did.

Smack! He closed his eyes on impact. Well, he'd stopped. That was for sure.

He opened his eyes. He was wedged between the boat and the large jetty support. The water swirled and raged around him. He desperately tried to keep his grip on the slippery pole, helped by the boat holding him there. Then the boat moved slightly. It was buffeting about in the racing tide, and at any second would likely bounce back against the support and crush him like an ant. Angus looked up and saw large staple-like prongs sticking out from the pole. A type of ladder he guessed. He grabbed at the lowest one and got his hand around it. The river pulled at him as though he belonged to it now and it didn't want to let go. Well, too bad for it. He hauled himself up just before the boat came crashing back in.

On the jetty, he collapsed with relief. He hadn't drowned. He hadn't been eaten by a shark. He hadn't been crushed to death by a luxury speedboat. He'd also avoided being beaten to a pulp by the Takani brothers. But he was dripping wet and a good couple of kilometres, he guessed, from the highway.

He stood up and felt his pocket. His wallet was gone. Washed away. Say goodbye to the money earned so far from his restaurant job *and* the money his parents had given him. Right now that meant that even once he made it back to the highway he'd have no money to catch the bus. It was going to be a long walk.

At the shore end of the jetty he took a narrow lane between two houses which led up to the street. He thought he might as well run if he could so he jogged along, his runners making wet squelching noises. Keeping the river on his left, he made it back to the highway after about fifteen minutes, pretty much dry thanks to the warm, sunny day.

Just before the highway there was a street off to the right which Angus realised must run along the back of The Sea Shanty. Might as well check out the back of the place while he was here, considering what he'd been through on this mission.

From this new perspective he could see that the back of the restaurant was attached to a larger, two-story building. It was an old motel. Run down and abandoned for some time, by the look of it. All the doors and windowsills had chipped paint that may once have been blue. Some of the doors were numbered; on others the numbers had either fallen off or were hanging at weird angles. He counted seven rooms on the ground floor and a set of stairs leading to the second floor with another seven rooms.

This rectangular block of rooms was joined to the back of The Sea Shanty by a smaller, square building (the old motel reception?) which sat at right angles to the other two, forming a three sided courtyard. The courtyard contained a wooden table and chair set, probably for the restaurant staff to use on breaks, and an industrial bin for garbage. From where he stood he could just hear music playing from the restaurant veranda over the noise of the clanging and banging from the restaurant kitchen.

A large faded sign sat in a patch of dead garden near the driveway. It read "The Ocean Wave Motel". In front of it was a brand new sign:

"FOR SALE: Redevelopment Opportunity. Prime Location." The number for a local real estate agent was listed.

Suddenly, a car screeched around the corner making Angus jump. It hurtled up the street and pulled to a stop at the curb on the other side. With the engine still running, the driver wound down the window and looked across at the restaurant/motel.

The driver was Dylan. Dylan the surfer jerk.

Angus took a slow step back in further behind the signs to hide himself.

The back door of the restaurant opened. The teenage waitress whom Angus had spoken to earlier came out. She spotted the car, waved, walked quickly over to it and got in the passenger door. Dylan and the waitress roared off up the street.

Interesting.

12 THE CIRCLE OF LIFE

"Your good luck charm doesn't work very well," said Hamish, shifting his laptop to the other arm. He, Angus and Bodhi were strolling toward the beach in the late afternoon sun. A weary Angus had made it back to the beach house just before four to see Hamish being dropped off by his parents. They were going out for a quiet dinner tonight, just the two of them.

Angus touched the fish hook around his neck. "You think?" he said.

"Not unless you call almost being beaten up and drowned in a river 'lucky'."

"I think you're wrong," said Bodhi. "The fish hook helped Angus to get away from Rapata and his brother and then kept him safe in the river."

The boys considered this. "I guess it all depends on how you look at it," said Angus, finally.

"So the cat said you'd be in danger three time, right? So, is that one or two?" said Hamish.

"Huh?" Angus said.

"Well, is the Takani brothers incident counted as the first danger, and the river the second danger? *Or* do you think they're both part of the same danger, meaning there are still two more to come?"

Angus shrugged. Bodhi said, "I'm counting it as two so far, *one* more to come. Angus was being dragged off to be beaten up by the Takanis. He got away. Then he jumped into the river. Entirely separate dangerous encounters."

"No," said Hamish. "He got away from the Takani's *because* he jumped into the river. You can't logically separate the two. They're part of the same dangerous incident, no doubt about it."

"Just so I'm clear," said Angus. "We're discussing

the finer points of a warning issued by…*a cat*."

Hamish put on a scary voice, "Take heed, Angus, and ignore the talking cat at your peril!" Angus laughed.

"Fair enough. Look, we're getting off track. We're supposed to be discussing the situation as it stands. The competition starts the day after tomorrow and we still have no idea where Leo is."

"Did you ask the cat?" said Hamish.

"Ha, ha," Angus said.

"Okay so what *have* we got then?" asked Hamish. They'd arrived at the seawall at Snapper Rocks. Angus summarised the situation as they climbed up onto the wall and got comfortable.

As it stood: Leo was favourite to win big prize money and a sponsorship deal but had disappeared; a printed note was found in his room, although he had no ready access to a printer; someone had drawn a doodle with red pen over his prized portfolio (he said he'd never go anywhere without) which they'd discovered had a Hawaiian meaning, 'circle of life'; in the garden near Leo's door had been found a napkin from The Sea Shanty, a reference to the surfing competition's prize money written on it in red pen; The Sea Shanty was attached to a closed-down motel, which was for sale;

Dylan Fraser, also competing in the competition, had been seen at The Sea Shanty with one of the waitresses. Angus paused in his summary to ask a question he wished he'd asked earlier.

"Who's likely to win if Leo doesn't compete?"

"Well," Bodhi said. "You have to remember that anything can happen on the day. Sometimes it depends on who gets the best waves. But...Dylan would have to be a good chance." They looked at each other as Hamish tapped on his laptop to start it up.

"Okay," said Angus, "and we know Dylan has an uptight father who's putting a lot of pressure on him to win."

"And don't forget he stole, or likely stole, Leo's surfboard from his family cabin. I mean, how did he know Leo wouldn't be there?" said Bodhi.

"And don't forget he's a jerk," said Hamish. "Okay, I've got Google up. What now?"

"Go to RealEstate.com and see if you can find the For Sale listing for the old motel," said Angus.

Hamish tapped for a bit. "Okay, here it is. Hmmm...prime location...developer's dream..."

"Does it say who owns it?" said Angus, impatiently peering over Hamish's shoulder. "It'll be under vendor details."

Hamish did a bit more tapping. "Okay, here it is," he said, finally. He looked up. "Crikey."

"What? What does it say," said Angus, fighting the urge to snatch the laptop from him.

"It says it's owned by a company called…Circle of Life Investments."

All three looked at each other.

"Circle of Life?" said Angus, feeling excited. "Well, there you go then."

"Huh?" said Hamish, "I'm a bit confused."

"It means," said Bodhi, "that someone *was* in Leo's room that night. Whoever it was drew the Circle of Life doodle on the portfolio and dropped the napkin outside."

"So who was it, then?" asked Hamish, his eyes popping.

"Google 'Circle of Life Investments'," said Angus. "Maybe we can find out more about it."

Hamish tapped away with the others peering over his shoulder. But no matter how much tapping was done, they couldn't come up with anything. Only that the company appeared to be owned by a complicated network of other companies. It was a dead end. Hamish closed the laptop.

"Let's go," he said. "I'm hungry."

They climbed down from the seawall and headed back to the beach house. No one said much on the way. Angus was too exhausted. And now frustrated. They were out of clues. There was nowhere left to go. Nothing more they could investigate.

They were almost at the beach house when Bodhi grabbed his arm and gave a sharp intake of breath. They were on the sidewalk right outside Rosa's Italian Café. Mr Mancini waved to them from inside.

"What?" asked Angus waving back.

"Look!" She was pointing up above the large glass doors at the Café sign.

"A sign. So?" said Hamish. Angus wasn't sure what she meant, either.

"Under the sign! Can't you see it?" she said. And then Angus did see it. Underneath the sign.

"A security camera. I can't believe I didn't notice it before," he said.

"So?" said Hamish, again. "There's a camera on the outdoor eating area. What's the big deal?"

"The big deal," said Angus, his spirits soaring, "is that opposite the eating area is our beach house. The camera is pointed right at Leo's door!"

"Whoever came to Leo's door that night would have been filmed by that camera," said Bodhi.

"Come on," said Angus, "Let's find out if Mr M still has the footage."

The three of them raced into the restaurant. Mr Mancini was busy setting tables. A delicious smell wafted from the kitchen. Yes, he still had the footage from Monday evening. It was all stored digitally on a hard drive and only deleted about once a month. He was sorry but he couldn't look at it with them right now. He had a busy night ahead, the café was booked out. But he promised they could look at it in the morning after Angus had finished his work.

"You want to take some pizza for dinner?" asked Mr Mancini.

"Thanks," said Angus, "but we're having the spaghetti you gave me this morning."

Bodhi grabbed Angus by the arm again.

"What now?" he said, looking at her.

"Pizza! Angus, tonight is the pizza-making competition. We forgot all about it! You're supposed to be at the surf club –" she looked at her watch, "in ten minutes!"

Angus groaned. He was beyond exhausted. Did he

really have to go and make pizza in a competition?

"I think I'll give it a miss," he said. "I'm too tired to be bothered with it."

"But you could win a surfboard," said Hamish.

That was true. Losing all his money in the river meant he wouldn't be *buying* one, that was for sure. Maybe he should go and make the pizza.

"Do it, Angus," said Bodhi. "We'll all come and watch. You'll win, I know you will. You're an awesome cook." Angus wasn't sure about 'awesome' but he did like to cook (it helped to have an ex-chef for a father), in fact, it was probably the only thing he could do better than Bodhi.

"Okay, let's go," he said.

"Wait!" Mr Mancini scurried to the kitchen and came back with a small, tattered looking book. "Angus, take-a this with you. It's my Rosa's recipes, bless her." He did the sign of the cross. "Pizza dough, page-a twenty-two. The best pizza dough. You win with-a this recipe. You are getting a surfboard, Angus, yes!"

Wow, this kind man trusted him with his dead wife's precious recipe book. "Gee, thanks, Mr Mancini," said Angus taking the old book. "I'll give this back to you in the morning, and I promise I'll take good care of it."

13 SURF'S UP

Fifteen minutes later, Angus took his place at the long stainless steel benches lined up in the surf club. He put on his apron. Hamish, Bodhi, Nate, and Mr Taylor were there with the other spectators watching on.

Angus looked down at his bench. On it were all the ingredients, bowls, trays and utensils necessary to make a pizza. He looked around. There were nine other kids each standing behind their own bench, most reading the dough recipe sheet provided by the club. Angus opened up Mr M's recipe book to page twenty-two and set it down on his bench. It looked like he was the only one not using the club's recipe.

The surf club President, who looked like an over-tanned middle-aged surfer, took the floor. Into his microphone he said,

"Welcome everybody to the inaugural Rainbow Bay Surf Life-Saving Club Kids' Pizza-Making Competition!"

The spectators clapped. Scanning the crowd, Angus was startled to see another familiar face. It was the waitress from The Sea Shanty, the one he'd seen getting into Dylan's car, here with a couple of other girls. They locked eyes and he saw hers widen in surprise and recognition. She got up from the table quickly and went out the door.

"Kids, here's how the competition will work. In front of you is everything you need to make your pizza. You will have twenty minutes to mix and knead your dough. Now, I'm no cook, ha ha," he turned and winked at the kids (confirming Angus's winking theory), "but they tell me that pizza dough needs to be left alone for a while to rise. So we'll let it do that for thirty minutes while we watch on the big screen, footage of some awesome surfing from last year's Quick Silver Pro Event. Then you will each return to your benches to roll your dough and add your toppings. Then into the ovens the pizzas will go!

"And don't forget, the theme of tonight's competition is 'Surf's Up'. The pizza deemed by the judges to be the most delicious, and which follows the 'Surf's Up' theme, will win this magnificent Firewire surfboard!" He waved his arm at the board displayed upon a table. "Tell me, what young surfer wouldn't be pleased to have this little beauty?"

Everybody clapped. The board was awesome.

Surf's up? Angus must have somehow missed that when he signed up. What could he do for 'Surf's Up?' Hawaiian ham and pineapple? No, too boring, surely?

The President continued. "Okay, kids. Let's get this dough made! You have twenty minutes. On your marks…get set…go!"

Okay, make the dough and worry about the topping later. Angus followed Mrs Mancini's recipe to a tee. He filled his bowl with warm water at the sink, (the recipe said NOT hot, NOT cold, but WARM), carefully measured out the exact amount of yeast, sprinkled it on top and stirred until it dissolved. Then he carefully measured out the flour, heaped it into a volcano shape (trying not to think about Bodhi being tossed into one) and poured in the yeast mixture and the precisely measured sugar, salt and oil. He mixed it all together. Now to knead.

Angus pushed and folded, pushed and folded, and pushed and folded, until the dough was smooth and elastic and his arms were ready to drop off. He put the dough into an oiled bowl and covered it with a tea-towel.

He collapsed on a chair next to Hamish to watch the surfing footage and wait for the dough to rise. He'd been the final contestant to sit down. Most of the others had kneaded their dough for only a few minutes. But Mrs Mancini's recipe stated quite specifically that the dough must be kneaded for *at least* fifteen minutes. Fifteen minutes was underlined.

"What are you doing for the 'Surf's Up' theme?" asked Hamish.

"I don't know," said Angus. "I hadn't realised until now that there *was* a theme."

"Well, that's not good," said Hamish. "All the others will have planned something, I would have thought. You should have planned something."

"Yes, Hamish," said Angus, irritably, "I should have

planned something. But in case you hadn't noticed, I've been a little busy trying to find a missing surfer."

"You'll be fine," said Bodhi, "Just channel your inner Italian. A surfing Italian."

The thirty minutes raced by and before he knew it, Angus was back behind his bench. Everyone had begun to roll out their dough and he still didn't have any idea what he was going to put on top of it. He began to roll hoping for an idea to come. As he rolled, his tired mind wandered to everything that had happened during the week. Leo going missing, the Hawaiian drawing, Mr Kahue and his talking cat –

Wait. Mr Kahue…

Angus pictured the old man bent over the workhorse, shaping a surfboard.

Of course, that's it! Angus rolled out his dough into a rough rectangle. Then he picked up a knife and began to carefully cut his dough out into a surfboard shape. What better for a 'Surf's Up' theme than a surfboard shaped pizza?

Now for the topping. He knew he wouldn't win with ham and pineapple even with the surfboard shape. They were at the famous Rainbow Bay so why not go with that? Angus finely diced some red, green and yellow capsicums (peppers) and began sprinkling it in arcs across the surfboard pizza to make a bright rainbow pattern. Then he added pink ham, white mushrooms and some pineapple *(why not?)* to his rainbow surfboard. A light sprinkling with mozzarella and he was done.

He stood back and admired his work. He was happy with it. It looked good. Maybe he *would* win the surfboard.

Hamish appeared in front of his bench.

"Wow," he said. "That's epic-looking!"

"Thanks," said Angus.

"I reckon you've nailed it," Hamish continued in a whisper. "I've checked out all the others. All their pizzas are boring circles. Mostly ham and pineapple. One kid's put broccoli on his. *Broccoli,* I'm not kidding."

Then it was time for the contestants to carry their pizza out to the kitchen for cooking in one of the three wood-fired pizza ovens specially brought in for the night. Angus stood in line, holding his pizza tray, waiting for his turn to put it into an oven. Things were delayed slightly when the assisting chef was called away to the phone.

Suddenly the kitchen's back door banged open. Dylan Fraser and the waitress stood there. Dylan's face was like thunder.

"That's him, there,' said the waitress, pointing at Angus. "That's the kid asking the questions."

Dylan strode over, grabbed Angus around the neck and pushed him up against the wall. Angus held tight to his pizza tray.

"I should have known it was you," he said. "Stop asking questions about Leo. If he doesn't want to compete that's his business. Stay out of it, you interfering brat! ARE WE CLEAR?"

Angus nodded as best he could with the hand around his throat. Why wasn't anyone helping him?

"Good," said Dylan. "Don't make me come back!" He took his hand away from Angus's throat and brought it smashing down onto the pizza tray. It went flying. The pizza fell to the floor. Dylan stomped on it, grinding it into the floor with his heel.

"Oops. Sorry," he said.

14 THE BLACK PORSCHE

Angus looked down at his ruined pizza as Dylan strode back out the door. People started to move. One of the other kids had finally thought to get some help. But it was too late.

"Oh my God! What happened?" Hamish and Bodhi were at his side.

"Dylan. That's what happened," said Angus. He looked at his friends. "I'm asking too many questions about Leo, apparently. He stormed in and smashed the pizza."

Everyone was speechless. This was too much. Angus didn't know whether to cry, be furious or both. Hamish, on the other hand, had no problem deciding. When he got angry his face turned red. Right now he looked like a beetroot.

"I've had enough of this guy. He can't push people around like that! I say we go after him and demand to know where Leo is. It's obvious he knows something. Come on!" Hamish was already making for the back door to follow Dylan.

"Hang on a minute!" called Angus, but Hamish was already out the door. Angus looked at Bodhi. "Come on," he said.

They ran out the back door and down the steps to the carpark where Hamish was scanning for Dylan.

"There he is!" Hamish pointed up the street at Dylan and the waitress. Angus grabbed his arm.

"Hold on a second! Confronting him won't work. He's not going to admit anything. Probably just threaten to hurt us. Let's just hang back and see where he goes."

"Angus is right, Hamish," said Bodhi. "Let's follow him."

"No!" said the still-red Hamish. "I'm gonna tell this

jerk what I think of him." He pulled his arm away from Angus and started walking fast up the street. Up ahead, Dylan and the waitress walked out to cross the road.

Before Angus could do anything, a car pulled away from the curb, quickly, just ahead of where he and Bodhi were standing. A black Porsche. Dylan and the waitress were now in the middle of the road. But they weren't looking back this way. The car accelerated straight toward them.

"DYLAN! LOOK OUT!" Angus yelled at the top of his voice.

Dylan's head spun around, he saw the car coming at him and pushed the waitress away. He tried to jump off the road himself but wasn't fast enough. The Porsche veered toward him, side-swiping him with a sickening thud. Dylan flew into the air and landed hard on the sidewalk as the car sped away.

Angus, Bodhi, and Hamish rushed to him. He was conscious, but groaning. There was a nasty gash on his forehead and his right leg stuck out at a weird angle. The waitress was screaming.

"Do you have a phone?" Angus tried to ask her, but she didn't seem to understand.

"I'll get help," said Bodhi and she dashed away back

to the surf club.

"Crikey," said Hamish, quietly.

***

The blue and red flashing lights made the street look like a weird disco as the ambulance loaded Dylan into the back. The police had taken statements from the three kids. Angus told how the Porsche had seemed to veer straight toward Dylan. And something else he'd noticed. The car hadn't had a registration plate. Not on the back, anyway.

As soon as the police were done with them, Mr Taylor took Angus, Hamish, and Bodhi back to the beach house. It was late, but since no one had eaten he heated up the spaghetti (without prawns) for everyone. Mr Parker had dropped by, sorry he'd missed the pizza competition. A warm evening, everyone was out on the deck again.

"I'm sorry to hear about what happened tonight, Angus, with the pizza and all," said Mr Parker. "Sounds like you were all set to win, too." He scratched his chin and said, "You know, Nate here has dozens of boards back home in the States. Nate, don't you have an old board here you could let Angus have?"

"You don't have to do that," said Angus. "I mean,

thanks, but really, it's okay."

Nate looked up. "Yeah, sure, Dad, I guess. I'll have a look at them tomorrow," he said, but without enthusiasm.

Mr Parker said, "Chin up, son. Leo might still show up to compete, you know. There's still a whole day to go." Then he added, "Or the kids might just find him for you. How's the investigation coming along, guys?"

"Great, now," said Bodhi. "The café across the street, where Angus works, has its security camera aimed right at Leo's door. After Angus finishes work tomorrow morning, Mr Mancini is going to let us look at Monday night's footage."

Hamish said, "If anyone did come to Leo's door that night, we'll know about it."

"Well, there you go, then," said Mr Parker. "Sounds like a plan. Angus, make sure you see Nate, here, tomorrow about that board, okay?"

Leaving the adults on the deck, the three kids went to the living room to drink hot chocolate and wait for Hamish's parents to pick him up.

With the adrenaline rush from the accident now wearing off, Angus could hardly keep his eyes open. What a day. He'd nearly been beaten up by Rapata, washed away in a river, spent an hour walking home, competed in a pizza-making competition and witnessed a guy getting hit by a car.

"So how many dangerous episodes is that now?" said Hamish, blowing on his chocolate.

"I still say it's just two," said Bodhi, before taking a sip. "Tonight was dangerous for Dylan, not Angus."

"What about when Dylan's hand was around his throat? Would the cat count that as dangerous?"

"Seriously, guys, forget about the cat," said Angus.

Bodhi laughed and said, "You know, Hamish, I've never seen you so angry. I think maybe Dylan was lucky the car got him before you did."

"Yeah, I'm like the Hulk," said Hamish. "If I get angry, you better look out."

"I don't like the Hulk, myself," said Bodhi. Hamish raised his eyebrows.

"Excuse me? Did you just say you don't like the *Hulk*? The most awesome Avengers superhero, like, ever? How is that even possible?"

"It's the anger thing. He's useless until he gets angry. What good is that? I mean, say you've got a problem and you need a superhero to help you. What good would it do calling the Hulk? How would you make him angry?"

"Poke him in the eye?" suggested Angus.

"But then he'd be angry at *you,* not whatever it was you needed help with," said Bodhi.

"I can't listen to this," said Hamish. "I won't sit here and let you run down the Hulk." Then he added, "You know, you're a lot more talkative than you used to be. I think I liked you better before." Bodhi grinned at him.

"She's right, Hamish," said Angus, yawning. "The anger thing is bad. No one makes good decisions when they're angry. The Hulk's a loose cannon."

"I'm going to pretend I didn't hear that," said Hamish.

"I don't particularly like Thor, either," said Bodhi, "but that's more about the stupid helmet than anything else."

"Well, I can't support you there," said Angus, stifling another yawn. "That's just crazy talk."

"So who *do* you like?" Hamish asked Bodhi.

Bodhi thought for a minute.

"Wasp," she said. "She's subtle. She gets the job done quietly with grace and style and without being all *'look at me and my big muscles'*." Then, with a twinkle in her eye, she added, "You know, the cat said I was graceful, when I was, you know, a Hawaiian Princess."

Angus was about to remind her that it was Mr Kahue that had said she was graceful, not the cat, but he fell asleep before he'd finished the thought.

15 ONE DAY TO GO

Angus woke with a start. It was morning. He was in his bed although he couldn't remember getting there. He looked at the clock on the bedside table. *7:20!* Oh, no, late for work with Mr Mancini!

He jumped out of bed, pulled on some clothes, and raced to the bathroom to splash water over his face and run a comb through his hair. Glancing at himself in the mirror he noticed dark circles under his eyes. He still looked tired. Oh well, he'd have to do. Trying to be quiet so as not to wake anyone, he carefully opened the front door, stepped outside, and silently closed it again.

"Angus," someone said from behind him. He jumped before realising it was just Mr Parker. He was standing in the drive, polishing his hire car with a cloth.

"Good morning. Hey, shouldn't you be at work?" he asked.

"I slept in."

Mr Parker laughed. "I'm not surprised."

"Yeah, well, I better get going. I'll see you later, Mr Parker."

"Sure, and don't forget to look at Nate's old boards today," he called as Angus dashed across the street.

The café's glass front doors were still shut. The place looked completely closed up which was odd because Mr Mancini was usually working by six in the morning. Something was wrong. Angus went around the back to the kitchen door and tried the handle. It was unlocked.

He pushed it open a bit, calling out, "Hello, Mr Mancini? It's me, Angus."

There was no answer. He pushed the door a little further. Then he smelt smoke.

Smoke?

He quickly pushed the door open all the way and

113

entered the kitchen. On the left was the little stairwell that led up to Mr Mancini's office and bedsit. It was filling with smoke.

There was a fire upstairs.

"Mr Mancini!" Angus shouted again, but received no answer. The smoke wasn't yet too thick. He grabbed a kitchen cloth from the counter and ran it under water at the sink. With the wet cloth over his nose and mouth he dashed up the stairs.

Mr Mancini was lying on his back in the narrow space between the office and the bedsit. He was unconscious but his chest was rising and falling. Breathing, at least. Smoke billowed from the office. Thick, black, choking smoke.

He had to get the fire brigade here, fast. He didn't want to run back downstairs to the phone and leave Mr Mancini – he might not get back up the stairs. And there was no getting into the office and using the second phone there.

Angus quickly stepped across Mr Mancini into the bedsit. He raced to the window and yanked it open, looking for Mr Parker across the street. Oddly, he wasn't in the driveway where Angus had left him. He was walking across the road, from the café side back to the beach house.

"Hey! Mr Parker!" shouted Angus. Mr Parker looked around. "Up here!" He waved his face cloth madly until Mr Parker spotted him. "The café's on fire! Call the fire brigade!" Mr Parker's expression changed from confusion to horror.

"Okay! Angus, get out of there!" he yelled, rushing toward the house.

Angus turned back to Mr Mancini. He couldn't just leave him here. You're not supposed to move unconscious people but he didn't have any choice. If he didn't get Mr Mancini downstairs now, the smoke would suffocate him before the fire brigade arrived. He tossed down the wet cloth. He could hardly hold it over his mouth and nose and carry Mr Mancini down the stairs at the same time. With great effort, he managed to get his hands under the man's armpits from behind and haul him up a bit. This was as good as it was going to get.

He dragged him toward the stairs. As a dead weight, the man was very heavy. But the flames were now licking the ceiling of the space out here and the smoke was thick. Angus started down the stairs. It was treacherous. He had to go down backwards while trying to drag Mr Mancini with him, his hanging legs and feet bumping at each step.

Finally, he made it to the bottom, dragged the older man over to the kitchen door and carefully laid him on the floor. He'd take him out the back to wait for the fire brigade. *Where were they, anyway?* He couldn't even hear sirens yet.

He turned the door handle. It wouldn't open. *What?* He tried again, desperately rattling it and pushing. It didn't budge. Angus had no time to dwell on why. Smoke as thick as soup was pouring down the stairs and filling the kitchen. He'd have to find another way out.

He picked Mr Mancini up under the arms again and dragged him into the dining area. At least there was less smoke here. For now.

Angus bent and put his cheek above Mr Mancini's mouth and nose. He couldn't feel any breath. The man had stopped breathing. Angus tried desperately to remember his first aid. He opened Mr M's mouth and checked for obstructions. Looked all clear. Then he tilted his head back by his chin to straighten his airway and noticed something. There was a wound on the side of his head. The hair there was matted with blood.

Angus breathed into his mouth twice and watched to see if his chest rose. It did. But then nothing again.

Angus continued to breathe into the man's mouth for what seemed like forever although it was probably about twenty seconds. Finally, Mr M's chest began to rise and fall on its own. Angus fell away with relief.

But it was short-lived. Noxious smoke was pouring from the kitchen into the dining area, filling it from the ceiling down. *Where was the fire brigade?* Keeping low to avoid the smoke, he rushed to the phone on the counter and put it to his ear. Nothing. It was dead.

Staying low, he ran to the large, glass front doors. Through them he could see across the street to the beach house. There was no one in sight. In desperation, and close to panic, he banged on the doors with his fists. They were still locked and he had no idea where the key was kept. Probably upstairs in the burning office. Angus coughed. The smoke was becoming unbearable. He looked at the umbrellas, closed and stacked neatly against the wall ready for setting up outside. He grabbed one. He already knew how heavy they were.

Doing his best to hold it like a battering ram he charged at the glass doors, screaming as he went.

"ARGHHHHHHH!" *CRASH!*

The glass shattered as the umbrella smashed through. Angus dropped it and picked up a chair to knock away

117

the rest of the glass as best he could. *Ahh! Blessed fresh air!* And finally he heard sirens. Flames were now shooting through the doorway from the kitchen into the dining area. Once again, he picked Mr Mancini up under the arms and dragged him out through the smashed front doors.

16 CRIKEY

Angus stood at the hospital window looking out. Down below, people were coming and going from the carpark. He watched an SUV pull in. It looked to be loaded with camping gear and had bicycles attached to the back. A tall, dark-haired lady parked it, jumped out and dashed towards the doors.

Angus took his seat again outside Mr Mancini's room. After being checked out himself, and given the all clear, he'd decided to wait here until there was some news about Mr M. Bodhi and Mr Taylor had begged him to come home with them, to get some much-needed rest, but Angus wasn't budging.

Of course, he wasn't allowed in to see Mr M as he wasn't family, but a kind nurse had taken pity on him and told him that he was still in a serious condition. He hadn't regained consciousness, and it was still unknown what the effects of his head wound might be.

Putting his face in his hands, Angus suddenly felt exhausted. This week was supposed to have been a fun holiday at the beach. It hadn't turned out that way. And he realised he hadn't called his parents like he'd told Mrs McLeod he would. A wave of intense home-sickness washed over him. He missed his mother and father, and his little brother, Liam. He wanted to go home. He'd tried to find Leo, but had failed. Any security camera footage was now burnt up in the fire and the competition was tomorrow. It was too late.

The dark-haired woman he'd seen in the carpark came bustling past with a nurse, looking upset. They went into Mr M's room and closed the door.

As weary as he was, Angus couldn't turn his brain off. There were still things about this whole mess that didn't make sense. Like, why had the kitchen door not opened when he'd tried to get Mr M out? Why had it taken so long for the fire brigade to come?

The whole thing with Mr Parker was a puzzle, too. In the end, he'd discovered, it was Mr Taylor, Bodhi's dad, who'd called the brigade after Bodhi had seen smoke pouring from the café. They said they hadn't seen Mr Parker that morning. He'd gone back to his hotel the night before, and as far as they knew, he hadn't returned.

Angus thought about him polishing the rental car in the beach house driveway. That was weird in itself. Who polishes a rental car? Well, maybe if you're trying to impress business contacts you might, he supposed. But, strangest of all, had been seeing him cross the street from the café to the house. What had he been doing? Again, Angus thought about the kitchen door that mysteriously couldn't be opened.

The dark-haired lady came out of the room. She stopped in front of him and smiled.

"They tell me you're Angus," she said in a kind voice. "Do you mind if I sit next to you?" Angus said he didn't and she took a seat. She told him her name was Gina, and she was one of Mr M's daughters.

"I'm really sorry about your Dad," said Angus. Gina shook her head.

"You've no reason to be sorry, Angus. From what I've been told, you saved Papa's life. They tell me there's nothing left of the café. If you hadn't carried him out of there he would have died." She put her hand on his shoulder. "You're a hero, Angus." With her other hand she wiped away a tear that trickled down her cheek. "Thank you," she said quietly.

"I...I...," Angus tried to speak, but truth was he didn't know what to say. He didn't feel like a hero. He'd just done what he had to do. And anyway, he had a sinking, sickening feeling that it was he who'd put Mr Mancini in danger in the first place.

"What will your father do without the café?" he said, finally.

"Oh, it was insured. He can rebuild it, don't worry. That's if *he* is okay, of course." She sighed and added, "Can you believe I'm supposed to be taking the kids camping? We were all packed up ready to go when I got the call. And now..."

"When will you know if he's going to be alright?" asked Angus.

"They don't really know. We have to wait for him to wake up."

Angus removed the fish hook necklace, the makau,

from around his neck and held it out to Gina.

"Could you give him this for me?" he said. "It's supposed to bring strength and good luck." Gina took the necklace. "I'm not too sure about the good luck part, though," Angus added.

Gina smiled. "Thank you, Angus. I will give it to him."

Angus then took from his pocket the little recipe book that Mr Mancini had given him for the pizza competition. "Here," he said. "Mr M said this was your mother's. He leant it to me and I was going to give it back to him this morning."

Gina took the book with wide eyes. "Mama's recipes," she said. Then she looked back at Angus. "I thought this was burned in the fire, like everything else." She hugged the book to her chest. Then she said, "If Papa leant you this it means you are someone special. Angus, my family is indebted to you. What can we do for you?"

Angus thought for a second. He'd been about to say, don't be silly, he didn't want anything. Instead he said, "Actually, do you have a phone I could borrow, please?"

Gina laughed. "Well, that's easy," she said and gave him her phone from her handbag. Angus thanked her and walked away to the window. He quickly called Hamish's mother and asked for Hamish.

"Angus! Crikey, I heard about the fire. Unbelievable! Are you alright?" Hamish babbled into the phone.

"Yes, I'm fine. Listen, can you Google Mr Parker, Nate's dad?"

"Um, yeah, I guess. But why?"

"Something's not adding up. See what you can find out about him. He's a rich business man so there should be plenty to find."

"Okay. Do you want to wait while I do it now?"

"No, I'm still at the hospital and I've borrowed this phone. I'll call you later from the beach house." He said goodbye and hung up.

He returned the phone to Gina and she went in to be with her father again. Angus sat back down. He felt queasy in the tummy and his head was spinning. He hadn't eaten yet today. He'd slept in and been in a mad rush to get to work forgetting to have breakfast. He rubbed his stomach.

Mr Parker couldn't really be a bad guy, could he? He'd been so kind and generous all week. Suddenly Angus felt guilty for asking Hamish to Google the man. Based on nothing more than a whim he was about to go sticky-beaking into his business. Maybe it was just time to accept he couldn't help Leo. Move on.

Back at the beach house he would call his parents and ask them to come get him. He had an overwhelming urge to sleep in his own bed tonight.

He went to get up but his stomach lurched. He was going to be sick. There was a bathroom not far up the corridor. He ran to it, pushed open the door, and raced into a stall. Leaning over the toilet bowl, his body kept trying to vomit but there was nothing in his stomach to come out. He stayed there until the cramps subsided. Then he splashed his face with water and tried not to look at himself in the mirror.

He came out of the bathroom and was about to turn toward the lifts when Gina came rushing up.

"Angus, they've been paging you," she said. "There's an urgent call for you."

A nurse at the station handed him a telephone. It was Hamish.

"Angus! You're not going to believe this," he said, "I couldn't wait until later to tell you."

"What?"

"Do you remember who owns The Sea Shanty restaurant and the old motel attached to it?"

"Yes, a company called Circle of Life Investments, so?" Angus said.

"Do you remember that we had no luck trying to find out anything about it?"

"Yes, of course, I remember. Get to the point, will you?" said Angus.

"Well, I've discovered who owns it."

"Who?" said Angus, then it hit him. "Not Mr Parker?" he said. It couldn't be.

"Mr Parker!" yelled Hamish. "He's a major shareholder of a company who owns *another* company that owns Circle of Life Investments, which means he also owns The Sea Shanty."

"But he told me he'd never heard of The Sea Shanty."

"He lied," said Hamish.

"Yes," said Angus. Mr Parker *had* lied to him, that much was clear. Could he have lied about other things, too? To Hamish he said, "Did you find out anything else?"

"Yes. You said he's supposed to be super rich. Well, guess what?"

"You're kidding," said Angus.

"No," said Hamish. "I'm *so* not kidding. He's not

rich. From what I've read, he *was* rich but has had a lot of business deals go wrong lately. Angus, he's in big financial trouble."

"Okay, thanks," Angus said, quickly, "I'll talk to you later." While Angus still had the nurse's phone, he dialled the beach house. Luckily, Bodhi answered.

"Bodhi, can you tell me quickly, with Leo *and* Dylan both out of the competition, who's likely to win?"

"Nate," she said without hesitation. "Nate, for sure. Angus – "

"Talk later, sorry!"

Angus hung up. It was Mr Parker. He was behind it all. And Angus now knew exactly where Leo was.

17 FINDING LEO

He raced back to Gina and explained to her what he wanted. It was urgent, he said. A life might depend on it.

"Of course, Angus," she replied.

Downstairs in the carpark, Gina took one of the mountain bikes from the back of her SUV and gave it and a helmet to Angus.

"Good luck," she said. "With whatever it is." Angus thanked her and took off. He'd been deliberately vague with Gina. If he'd told her what he suspected, she might have insisted he get the police and Angus didn't think they'd do anything. He didn't have any hard evidence against Mr Parker. Time was running out. There was nothing for it but to check it out himself.

He pedalled furiously toward The Sea Shanty and the old motel. Leo was being kept prisoner in one of the abandoned rooms, Angus was certain of it. That's if he was still alive.

Mr Parker had tried to kill Dylan by running him over. And he'd set fire to the café after hitting Mr Mancini on the head, Angus felt sure of it. So, it was possible that Leo was already dead.

He willed his legs to go faster but it was like he was in a dream and everything was going in slow motion. And, of course, he got every red light on the way. Normally, Angus would follow all the road rules carefully but today he cut a few corners, literally. He raced through one intersection and was nearly run down by a bus which honked at him angrily. Okay, calm down. No sense in getting run over, too.

After what seemed like a hundred years, he turned into the street that ran behind The Sea Shanty and the adjoining old motel, and then swung into the drive. Even though it was still too early for the restaurant to be open, loud rock music pumped from the kitchen. The staff would be preparing for lunch service.

Angus dumped the bike and ran to the ground floor of the old motel.

"Leo! Leo, are you in there?" he called, forcing himself to move slowly along the seven downstairs rooms so as not to miss anything. At each one he tried the door handle. All were locked. Each room had a window. Some still had curtains that were firmly closed. The ones without curtains appeared to be empty. When he came to the end of the row he noticed something he hadn't seen before. A shed, tucked in behind the old reception area.

"Leo? Where are you?" he called, walking around it. It had a high window. Angus pulled a chair from the outdoor setting over and climbed up on it.

In the shed was a black Porsche. His heart rocketed to his throat. Mr Parker had tried to kill Dylan by running him over. There was no doubt now.

Angus leapt down from the window and raced up the stairs to the top row of motel rooms. Leo had to be here somewhere. The doors were on his right. The other side of the walkway was bordered by a chest high railing. He could see through it to the courtyard below. He moved along the row, again trying door handles and calling out for Leo. He got to the last room. Nothing. He felt defeated. What could he do? He couldn't bash all the doors down. He leant against the red fire alarm box attached to the end wall. He had to think. An awful smell wafted up from the industrial-sized garbage bin below.

Then he heard something.

Knocking.

Someone was knocking from inside the last room! It was down low on the wall and difficult to hear over the music. His heart did a backflip.

"Leo? Leo is that you?" he called.

The knocking came more quickly.

"Leo, it's Angus. If that's you, knock twice."

Two knocks came. Angus wanted to shout for joy but instead said, "Knock twice if you're tied up."

Two more knocks.

Angus rattled at the door handle furiously but it was useless.

"Okay, Leo, I'm going to get the police. I'll get you out. Don't worry!"

But as Angus turned to run to the stairs, Mr Parker's silver rental car pulled into the driveway, running straight over the top of Gina's bike. Angus ran for his life toward the stairs, knowing he'd be trapped if he didn't get down, but Mr Parker jumped out of the car and was at the bottom before he could get there.

"Hi, Angus. What's the rush?" Mr Parker was smiling up at him with his friendly smile, hands on hips.

Angus glanced back along the walkway. There was nowhere to go. The stairs were the only way down and Mr Parker stood firmly at the bottom of them.

The man held up his hands.

"It's not what you think, Angus. Come on down here now, and we'll talk this through."

Angus stayed where he was, trying desperately to come up with a plan. He could try yelling for help but no one would hear it over the kitchen's loud music.

"Do as you're told, now, boy," said Mr Parker, still smiling. "This is none of your concern. Come on down here."

"You kidnapped Leo," Angus said. He was trying to stall for time as much as anything else. "The next morning you pretended you'd just come from the airport but you were already here, weren't you?"

"You need to understand, Angus. I just need a little extra cash, right now. Nate has to win that competition tomorrow, that's all."

That's all?

"And you tried to kill Dylan. Did he know you'd kidnapped Leo?"

Mr Parker laughed. "That nasty little jerk wouldn't know if his own butt was on fire. No, he was just strutting around enjoying the fact that Leo was missing. And he certainly didn't want him found, now did he? With Leo gone, he thought he could win. I couldn't let that happen, now could I?"

"You slashed the tyres on the car so we couldn't drive up to the cabin. You didn't want us finding out that Leo wasn't there."

"Didn't count on you taking the bus, though, did I?" Mr Parker smirked. "I hadn't realised then what a determined young man you are. When I heard you'd taken the bus I tried to get there ahead of you, put some food in the place, make it look like Leo was there. But you beat me to it."

Angus remembered the bag of groceries he'd seen in the man's car. Then he thought of something else that made him feel sick.

"You hurt Mr Mancini. You hit him on the head and set fire to his café. And then you locked me in there, didn't you?"

"Don't take it personally, Angus. But you were about to ruin everything with those security tapes. I couldn't let that happen so I wedged a piece of timber up under the door handle. Besides, you should've been in there already. I didn't count on you being late for work."

"Is Nate in on it?"

Mr Parker's face clouded over. "Nate knows nothing. And we're going to keep it that way. I need him to do well tomorrow. Now, I've just about had enough of this. I'm coming up." He put his other foot on the bottom step.

Angus turned and ran. He heard Mr Parker pounding up the stairs after him. He raced along the walkway. He had one chance. As he neared the end wall he lifted his fist and smashed it as hard as he could into the glass fire alarm box, praying that it still worked.

An ear-piercing bell shrieked through the air. It was still connected! The alarm was going off. That would bring people, surely?

He turned. Mr Parker was at the top of the stairs. His face was crazy.

"Why, you little…" There was something black and shiny in his hand. *A gun?* He charged at Angus.

Angus swung himself up on the railing and leapt.

18 YOU STINK

With a squelchy thud, he landed on the bags of garbage in the industrial bin. Ugh! Rotten seafood. Over the pealing alarm, he heard voices, then yelling. Then an engine started up and a car screeched away. He tried to stand up but it was difficult inside the bin with the soft garbage bags beneath him.

"Help!" he shouted, "I'm in here!"

A man wearing a chef's hat peered over the side of the bin. "What the…?" he said, looking at Angus.

"Call the police," said Angus. "Quickly."

***

Angus, Bodhi, and Mr Taylor watched on as Leo was loaded on a stretcher into the back of an ambulance. He appeared to be okay, all things considered. Before they closed the doors, he gave Angus a smile and a thumbs up.

A burly police-sergeant came over to the group.

"They're going to check him over at the hospital, but it looks like he'll be okay. Says Parker came to his room Monday night, they chatted for a bit and then Parker pulled a gun on him. He's spent the last five days tied up and gagged, but Parker came every day to give him food and water."

"Will he be able to compete tomorrow?" asked Angus.

"Depends on how he feels, I would think, and what the docs say. But if he does, he'll have you to thank for it." The sergeant was called away by another cop waving a radio.

"Well done, Angus," said Mr Taylor. "I should have listened to you kids from the beginning. Thank goodness you knew to keep following your instincts. I still can't believe it. I've known Nate's dad since the boys were little. I never would have thought…"

"It still doesn't really make sense," said Angus. "Why would he keep Leo alive yet try to kill Dylan and then Mr Mancini and me?"

Bodhi answered. "I think he's crazy. Seriously. First of all, the prize money was never going to be enough to get him out of his money problems. But I think he was desperate. And he became *more* desperate as the week went on, especially as he realised you were on to him."

"I wasn't really on to him," said Angus. "Not until right at the end."

"No, but he knew you were following the clues and that you'd eventually work it out," said Bodhi.

"He might not have been trying to kill Dylan, you know," said Mr Taylor. "Just hurt him enough so that he couldn't compete. But I think he totally lost the plot last night when you guys told us about Mr Mancini having video footage. I think you're right, love," he said to Bodhi, "he got crazier as Angus got closer."

"Well," said Bodhi, "I can tell you that Angus is way too close right now. Seriously, dude, you *stink!*"

"What?" said Angus, "Don't you think rotten seafood would make a nice cologne?"

The police-sergeant came back over. "We've got

him," he said. "At the airport, trying to get out of the country."

19 EPIC!

"Hamish! You need more sunscreen, lad, come here!" called Mrs McLeod in an enormous floppy hat, and brandishing a tube of sunscreen. Angus laughed as Hamish was chased around by his mother. They were on the beach, at Snapper Rocks, watching the tail end of the rookie competition. Leo was out there on his prized Forget-Me-Not. Of course, he'd made it through the heats easily and was about to pick his final wave.

"Been a big week, hey, mate?" Angus's father put his

arm around his shoulders and squeezed.

"Yeah, Dad," Angus said, looking up at his father. It was so great to have his family here. After the competition they were going to pack his things at the beach house and head home. On his other side, his mother took her phone away from her ear, took his hand and gave it a little squeeze.

"So proud of you, love," she said. "That was Gina. Mr Mancini has woken up. He's going to be fine after some bedrest. We'll bring you back to visit in a couple of days."

"Oh, thank goodness," said Angus, returning the squeeze.

"And, by the way, I heard a whisper that a certain someone is about to be nominated for a bravery award, which is just terrible, of course."

"*A bravery award*, really? Me? You're kidding? Wait. Why is that terrible?"

"Because, I have nothing to wear to Government House." She tousled his hair.

"Angus! Come and ride the boogie board with me!" said his brother, dancing around him.

"Okay, in a minute, Liam. I want to watch this, first."

Suddenly the PA system blared into life. Leo was up

on his final wave. It was an incredible right-hander, easily eight feet. He dropped down the face, did an awesome bottom turn and then carved it up. He was all speed, power and technical skill, culminating in the most epic 360 aerial Angus had ever seen. He must have gotten six feet of air. *Woot!* That'd be a ten, for sure.

The crowd went off.

***

Thirty minutes later, Leo was up on the podium accepting his trophy, grinning from ear to ear. The photographers and news crews were going wild. The story was sensational, of course. Missing pro surfer kidnapped and held captive for five days only to be rescued in time to win the title. A newsroom's dream.

Leo took the microphone.

"Ah...I don't want to say anything until the person responsible for me being here today is up here with me. Angus, where are you, mate?" Leo scanned the crowd.

"Here he is, here he is!" shrieked Liam, jumping up and down. The crowd all turned to stare at Angus.

"There you are. Come on up here, buddy," Leo said into the mike.

"Go on, mate," Dad said in his ear and Bodhi gave him a little push from behind.

Oh gosh, this was embarrassing. Angus had no choice but to push through the crowd toward the podium. The photographers began snapping photos of *him*. He wondered vaguely if he still had circles under his eyes.

When he finally made it to the podium he took Leo's outstretched hand and was pulled up. He stared out at the thousands of people on the sand.

"Everyone, this is Angus Adams, the most awesome kid I know. Like I said, I'm only here today because this guy didn't give up on me." The crowd clapped and cheered their approval.

"I have no doubt that, if he wants it, he'll one day be accepting this trophy himself. In the meantime, help me hold it up, mate."

Angus held one side, Leo the other, and together they hoisted the trophy into the air. The crowd and photographers went nuts.

It was epic.

They lowered the trophy and Leo hugged him.

"Thanks, dude," Leo said in his ear. "I owe you one."

***

Trying to get back to the beach house was a struggle with his parents fending off photographers and reporters, all keen to get a photo or a comment. In addition, his parents' phones had been ringing nonstop with TV stations offering deals for his exclusive story.

But all Angus wanted to do was go home.

"Thanks for having me, Mr Taylor," he said to Bodhi's dad when they were ready to leave.

"No worries, mate. Anytime," said Mr Taylor. "Oh, by the way, Nate left something for you. It's out by the car."

Angus followed him outside. Nate had flown back to the States to be with his mother as soon as he'd learned what his father had done. He'd said he couldn't even think about competing.

"He wants you to have this."

It was his surfboard. His best one. A Fred Rubble, like Kelly Slater used. This was too much.

"I...I can't take this," stammered Angus. "It's worth way too much."

"He wants you to have it. And he left you this, too." Mr Taylor handed Angus a note. He opened it up. It read:

Angus,

Take the board. Please. I can't bear to look at it and I have heaps more, anyway. I'm sorry about everything.

Keep eating those macadamia nuts, dude. Best, Nate.

***

They had the board strapped to the top of the car, and Angus's bag in the back when Hamish and his parents pulled up. They were heading home, too, but Hamish wanted to say goodbye first.

"See you back at school," he said as Angus climbed in the car and wound down the window.

"The cat was way off, you know," Hamish added. "You were in danger at least five times by my count."

Angus grinned. "I'll be sure to let Mr Kahue know." His dad started the engine.

"Just be glad you're not a Hawaiian Princess," called Bodhi as the car edged away from the curb. "You think you've had it hard? Try being thrown into a volcano!"

From up the street, Angus stuck his head out of the window and yelled back, "WASN'T THAT THE AZTECS?"

HAVE YOU READ ALL OF THE FREE-RANGE KID MYSTERIES?

Angus Adams and the Free-Range Kid Mysteries
(Book 1)
Angus Adams and the Missing Pro Surfer (Book 2)
Angus Adams and Scream House (Book 3)

Email Lee. M. Winter: lee@leemwinter.com

52648942R10095

Made in the USA
Lexington, KY
05 June 2016